second time around

Potter Lake Small Town Romance
Book Two

dl white

books by dl white

second time around

one

. . .

SAGE

"There you go, Mayor Cavanaugh. Sorry about the wait. I had to hand steam the milk."

Sage Owens, owner of Rooster's Coffee, slid a frothy medium latte across the counter and smiled up into the handsome face of Potter Lake's new mayor.

Well, the term *new* was relative. The previous Mayor, Quincy Adams, had been in office for as long as anyone could remember because no one had had the guts to run against him. He was scamming half the town and trying to put the other half out of business, so Kade Cavanaugh had done just that, and won by a landslide. Last anyone heard from Quincy, he tucked tail, vacated the official residence, and moved to Birmingham, Alabama. Good riddance.

"Not a problem," he said, lifting the thick paper cup to sip a bit off the top. He licked froth from his lips and hummed his approval. "Mmmmm, that's good. And I keep telling you to call me Kade. Or KC. We're colleagues."

Though he spent most weekdays running Potter Lake, a few evenings a week, Saturdays and holidays, you could find Mayor Cavanaugh at Guys N' Dolls Salon. Since City Hall was likely closed for the Christmas holidays, he had been spending a lot of time at the shop, trying to give his hard-working barbers and the manager — his sister, TC — some respite.

Sage shook her head, planting a fist on her hip. "And I keep telling you that my MaDear would come up out of her grave to shake her finger at me calling the mayor by his first name. You're just going to have to get used to it. It's that or *Your Honor*."

Mayor laughed, a hearty and loud guffaw. "Oh no, no, no. I can't even… no." He reached for a lid and snapped it on top of his cup, then pushed his wallet into the back pocket of some loose athletic pants with the *Aria* logo printed down the side. The black shirt he wore matched, with Aria in neat printing across the right front breast. Back in his NBA days, that was the brand he represented and though he hadn't seen a court in years, he still wore it proudly.

"Thanks Sage. Appreciate it." He squinted as he turned to stare out of the windows of the shop. Her end of the parking lot was so empty, Sage swore she saw a tumbleweed blow through. "It's strange that business is so slow today."

"Must be the weather. Or the holiday. Is the barbershop busy?"

"Always. And Leslie's back-to-back at the Curl & Dye this morning. People trying to get fine for Christmas, I guess. Speaking of busy, I'd better get back. If you get lonely, come on down to Guys N Dolls."

"I just might do that. You got that cute baby over there today?"

He moved toward the door, but not before beaming a proud grin. Little KJ was a bright ray of sunshine, a perfect mix of Leslie and Kade. "Not this morning, but Leslie will probably bring him by later on. I'll text you."

Sage waved as he swung the door open and headed down the sidewalk to his end of the row. *Rooster's Coffee* and *Guys & Dolls* bookended the line of shops in the ever-expanding strip mall. Every time she turned around, something new was being built, or somebody was having a grand opening.

The Potter Lake population exploded when Mayor Cavanaugh took over and started making good on his promises to improve the town. His goal was to make Potter Lake a friendly small town, and they were well on their way. Streetlights and wide sidewalks had been added, and a trolly that would take you from one end of the town to the other and back again. He even established bus service to and from Healy so that people could easily live and work in either town.

Sage still liked Healy exactly where it was, twenty miles west, but it was nice to ride out and spend a day shopping, see a movie, and visit with her daughter, Rae.

She was a senior at Healy University, and a major reason that she had sold her house and moved from Ocala, Florida to Georgia. Gordon, her husband, had only been gone a little over a year when Rae left for college and Sage missed her every second of every day. She was miserable, alone, and lonely. Over spring break that year, Rae talked about a little town about twenty miles away from the college. It was growing quickly, she said, and the mayor was talking about getting people to move out there and start up a business. Maybe Sage could do just that and open that little coffee shop she had talked about for years.

It wasn't like Sage didn't have the money. Gordon's life insurance and careful financial planning had them covered, and then some. Sage still wanted a life — she couldn't just sit in the house and watch the time pass. She could do whatever she wanted to do. And what she wanted to do was to be near her daughter. So, excited, she listed the house and started packing and made trips back and forth, looking for merchant space and a home.

For the first year, she lived in an apartment close to Rooster's, but it seemed so modern. Contemporary. She wanted something older, something… country, with a little character. Then the perfect place opened up, a garage apartment that a member of her church had posted for rent. Her daughter, the previous tenant, had moved in with the man who would later become the mayor.

Sage checked her watch, then rounded the counter to stand at the window and take in a long glance at the empty parking lot. It looked like most of the shops were doing little to no business. Except for Guys N' Dolls, which always seemed to be hopping, mostly because it was as much a hangout spot as it was a family salon. It was a good thing that business was slow, because the espresso machine had been broken for two days and calls to Brevel to send the repairman back out seemed to go unanswered.

A small, white pickup that had seen better days turned into the parking lot. It crawled past the shops between Rooster's and Guys N Dolls, then pulled into the space in front of the entrance. Sage stepped back from the window and watched him slowly, bit by bit, get out of the truck.

One boot hit the ground, and then the other. A pair of dark jeans was visible in the space underneath the driver's side door while he leaned into the cab of the truck and grabbed what looked like a small clipboard. He straightened, then stepped back, then slammed the truck door shut, the vehicle seeming to shudder with the impact.

A button-down shirt was open at the collar, covered by a black zip-up hoodie with *Alexander Repair* embroidered across the breast. He was tall; not a giant like KC, but tall enough to lift her gaze as he approached the front door. His legs were long, his gait smooth. His clean-shaven face had a strong chin, high cheekbones, and enviable lashes and brows.

This… wasn't her usual repairman. Ned drove a flashy fire engine red Dodge Ram, was short and stocky and had a belly that made him look like he was in his third trimester. Sage realized she'd been standing in the window, staring in time to reach out and open the door for him. He smiled as he stepped inside.

"Are you Sage Owens? I'm from Brevel."

"I'm Sage, yes," she answered, without swooning over the baritone sounds that seemed to come from the depths of his chest. "What happened to Ned?"

He reached into a pocket to show her a plastic encased ID card. "Bennett Alexander," he said, then tucked it away, bringing up the clipboard. "I'm with Alexander Repair. I have no idea where Ned is, but I've taken over his customers in this area. Everybody's been asking and everybody's mad 'cause they haven't seen him."

Sage huffed. "Yeah. My machine has been down for days, and I haven't heard a peep. Thought I was going to have to get ugly with Brevel. I pay a maintenance contract on this thing for a reason." She turned, waving at him to follow. "It's this one here."

"And what is it doing? Or not doing?"

"Steaming. I can get hot coffee, no problem, but if I need froth or to steam milk, I have to use that hand steamer over there." I pointed to the small, discarded appliance on the counter.

"Gotcha." He took in the shiny silver contraption with all its bells and whistles that rendered the unit useless if the bells and whistles didn't work. "I'm going to grab my toolbox and I'll open her up and take a look."

Sage watched his long-legged stride out of the shop and wondered, almost aloud, about this new repairman. He wasn't young by any stretch of the imagination. But he wasn't an old man, either. Seasoned, as the kids say. Stocky, but not rippling with muscle. Smooth, dark skin, smoky brown eyes, and only a hint of silver in the low-cut hair on his head.

In nearly the same moment, she chided herself. *Looking at some man like he's tonight's dinner. But a delicious dinner he would be...*

Bennet came back in, toting a medium sized metal box. "Mind if I set this here?"

Sage nodded. He set the box down on the faux marble counter, then reached behind the machine and flipped the switch to turn it off, then flipped the hinges at the side to swing open the face of the unit. All her inner workings were on display for the world to see.

"How long have you had this unit?"

"Just a couple of years," she answered, leaning against the counter to watch him work.

She never watched Ned work. In fact, Sage preferred to not even be in the same room as Ned. He'd talk nonstop to anyone in hearing range, usually about nothing that made any sense. Or sports, even though she had told him a hundred times that she wasn't a sports watcher.

Bennett, though... she watched those nimble fingers dig into the machine and take the bits and pieces apart and set them on the counter all in a line.

"Was it new when you bought it?"

"Aw no, used. This place has only been open about three years. I'm new out here."

"Me too. Brand new," he replied, lifting his head up and out of the machine. "Brevel asked if I'd be willing to take over this territory. I needed a change of pace, so I figured, why not? I guess it saves the time of having to send someone from twenty miles away, huh?"

Sage bobbed her head, absentmindedly nodding.

"I'm renting a spot until I get things squared away, but I'm thinking I might buy one of those new houses they're building. Then again, I hear there's some nice land on the other side of the lake. More room to do what you want without having neighbors in your business."

"I just moved into a place over on the other side. I prefer it."

He brightened, smiling while turning a screwdriver. "Oh yeah?"

"Have you met Leslie? The mayor's wife? She owns the Curl & Dye Beauty Shop over there."

"Everybody knows Leslie. I rewired two of her hair dryers last week. And I was a serious fan of her husband back in the day."

"Well, I'm renting her old place. It's a little apartment over the garage at her folks' house, just what I needed. And now and again, Lee — Leslie's mama? She'll make a few dozen treats for me to bring to the coffee shop to sell."

"I'm sure they're good. I've heard about her carrot cake." The screw he'd been fighting finally gave, granting him entrance to another part of the machine. "I think I see the problem. Got a kink in your line. That happens in these refurbished units with the old steel parts. And looks like your temperature gauge is about gone. Have you been having issues with it?"

Sage nodded, proceeding to go into what was probably a long, boring story about how long it took to get a decent cup of steamed milk or stiff peaks of foam. "So how long am I going to be down? Is there any way to rush the parts? That hand steamer is going to be the death of my wrist."

He smiled, showing off a pretty white set of teeth. "Ms. Owens, when I walk out of here, this machine is going to be pumping out more lattes than you can handle."

Sage tried hard not to grin like an idiot, but she couldn't help it. His voice was so... deep and yet silky smooth. "Please, call me Sage. And wow, really? Ned always had to order parts, and they took forever to come in and then he'd have to come back, and charge me for the return—"

"Sage?" He cut her off with a warm hand on her shoulder. "You will not see Ned ever again. This machine is mine now, and I'm going to take excellent care of her."

"Well alright, Mr. Bennett Alexander. I'd best let you get to work."

two

. . .

BENNETT

Bennett walked out of the shop toward his truck, shaking his head in absolute amazement. This "Ned" was an idiot and a thief, dragging out service calls so he could double bill. He was probably overcharging on parts, too. There was no reason not to keep small replaceable parts on your truck and fix things on a single visit. To get over on any of your customers, specifically a woman who was trying to do something for herself, was reprehensible. His mother took in laundry and did sewing most of his childhood, so he knew the heartache that having a machine breakdown could cause. It would put a serious limp in her stride.

His phone buzzed in his pocket as he stood at the back of the truck, sifting through the crates of small parts and miscellaneous tools. It was an organized mess, functional to no one but Bennett. He pulled the device out to glance at the screen and smiled, pressing the button to accept.

"Hi Daddy," came the tinny sound of his daughter,

Rebecca. "I have Albert here. We were just calling to see what you were doing."

"I'm working, but not for long. I'm on my one and only call. Going to go get a haircut, see what's going on with the fellas. You uh…. you and Albert get that favor done for me?"

"Yes, Daddy. We got the flowers and put them on her grave. I'll text you a picture when we hang up. So you're good?"

Bennett considered the question, weighing his emotion and general outlook of the day. He decided he felt pretty good.

"I'm better than I thought I would be. But I'm on a service call, so let me call you back later—"

"It's okay, dad." Albert's low baritone came through, sounding like he was hovering a few inches from the phone. "I have to pick up a couple of things for grandma for dinner tomorrow. Are you sure you'll be okay spending Christmas alone? We can fly you here. Don't worry about the cost."

"Naw, naw. I'm fine. I'm looking forward to it. Something new, you know?"

"Yeah. Well, if you insist that you're fine—"

"And I do."

"—then I guess we'll talk to you tomorrow. Love you, dad."

"Love you too, ladybug. You too, son. Talk to you tomorrow."

"Yeah, Dad."

He disconnected the call and slid the phone back into the pocket of his zippered hoodie. He gathered the parts and tools needed and headed back to the coffee shop.

Bennett hadn't planned on working today. He had long ago scheduled the day off but when Brevel called and said they had an emergency and said where it was, he'd taken the call. He could use the distraction.

Today was Virginia's birthday. Her fifth birthday since

she'd passed, and he still woke up out of a dead sleep on December 24th, panicking because he hadn't picked up the flowers or a card or anything, and he knew she'd be upset because he'd forgotten. Virginia had been one of those kids that got presents for both holidays wrapped up in one. Bennett made it a point to celebrate her birthday separately. One full day to celebrate Virginia Alexander.

After he remembered that she was gone and probably wouldn't be already counting the minutes of her full day of celebration, he laid back down. He wasn't even in Charlotte this year. The kids would take care of the flowers for him.

He couldn't go back to sleep, though. He just… lay there on his back, staring at the ceiling fan until sunrise. Then beyond sunrise. Then he got the service call and figured that if he didn't get out of bed, he would lie in it all day.

Sage was right where he had left her, leaning against the counter. "Sorry about that. My kids were calling from back home."

"Kids?" Her eyebrows shot up toward her hairline. Bennett saw her sneak a peek at his left hand and the glimpse of confusion at the presence of no ring. "You have kids?"

"Two grown ass crumb snatchers. They're twenty-one and twenty-three."

"Oh." She sighed a light breath, then laughed. "I thought you meant babies. My Rae is twenty-two. Seems like they were just babies, though, doesn't it?"

"Sure does. I feel like it was just yesterday that Virginia was pacing and cursing, and I was timing contractions." Bennett bent to look into the machine, thinking he could easily replace the line and the broken temperature gauge. He liked when he felt like I was doing something for someone. Providing a service, making things better, righting a wrong. The ones he could right, anyway.

"So, did your wife move with you, or…"

The question, one he was expecting, trailed off at the end.

Bennett's foray into dating after having been married for so long came in very short spurts, but they'd taught him to pick up on the nuances of the single woman. They would often hint at a wife, girlfriend, or life partner, just to feel out the situation. Sometimes, if he didn't want to be available, he told women that he was married but didn't wear a ring because of his job.

So, Bennett had to decide, at that moment, if he was available. Sage was a nice-looking woman, comfortable in a pair of curve hugging leggings, a red rooster's coffee t-shirt and a pair of loafers. Not anyone that would grace the cover of a magazine, but how real were those women, anyway? He was attracted to a woman's soul, her kindness to others, her openness, her spirit. But Sage's pretty walnut skin, a figure he could imagine wrapping his arms around, short sassy hairdo, big almond-shaped brown eyes and full lips weren't any hardship to look at.

Besides, Bennett didn't see a ring on her finger, either. She wouldn't be asking about a wife if she had a husband. Right?

He straightened, dropping the dented and corroded pipe on the counter next to the machine. He reached for the new clear plastic cylinder, still in its packaging, and tore it open. "No. My uh… my wife is gone. Five years now. Breast cancer, metastatic. Took her pretty quickly."

Bennett avoided looking at women when he informed them of his marital status. *Widower.* He didn't know how to act, what to do with his face when he gave the brief rundown. Was she supposed to be happy to hear about the demise of the love of his life? If she was, would that be a… turn off? Was that a red flag? He couldn't grasp it himself.

A low moan and sucking of teeth, however, drew his attention to Sage. Her expression was sad. But also… something else.

"My husband, Gordon, died five years ago. Car accident,

real bad. He lived for a few days, but…" She bowed her head, her eyelashes fluttering with her rapid blinking.

"I'm sorry to hear that. Really sorry to hear that."

After a few quiet moments, her head lifted. Her eyes were glassy, but not a tear had fallen. "Thanks. I know you know how I'm feeling."

"Yeah." Bennett nodded, then went back to work on the machine. "I finally moved away because, you know, everyone knew us. I felt like I was being reminded, all the time, about what we had. Places she loved to go, dishes she loved to eat, even the building she worked in. I had to drive past there every day and not stop in and say hey, take her to lunch. The kids are gone, away at college. I just—"

"Needed a new start. Yeah."

Sage shifted her weight from one leg to the other, glancing out of the window at the empty parking lot, her arms folded across her ample chest. "I moved out here to be close to my daughter. Got her enrolled at college, then found a little something for me to do. I just couldn't sit around, missing him anymore."

Bennett straightened again, this time affixing his full attention on her. "So you really feel where I'm coming from."

"Yep. This little town has been a lifesaver, though. Friendly people, a real small-town atmosphere. Very welcoming, like family."

"I definitely agree with you there. They have surprised me."

With a quick twist of a screwdriver, he had swapped out the temperature gauge and tossed the old one on the counter. He closed the front door to the machine and reached behind it to flip the power switch. It buzzed and hummed and beeped, coming to life.

"You get good business here?"

"Usually. I'm surprised we're so dead right now. Must be

the weather and the holiday. We're usually hopping. Maybe the after work rush."

"Well…" Bennett paused, watching the machine adjust and bring itself to normal working order. "What do you say we give this thing a whirl?"

Sage grinned, beaming a beautiful smile in his direction. "Okay! Do you drink coffee? Whaddya have, on the house?"

"Oh. Lemme do like… a caramel latte. Sounds good."

"Alright," she said, practically bouncing across the room to grab a cup and the ingredients she needed to make his coffee. "Let's take her for a spin."

three

. . .

SAGE

The latte Sage made him could probably win first place in the Best Latte Ever Awards, if those existed. She was precise, slowly, methodically going through her paces. Coffee. Syrup. Milk. Froth — which, by the way, was perfect.

Bennett sipped slowly, since it was probably scalding hot. "I'll have to adjust to having a working temperature gauge. Sorry it's so hot."

"It's alright. It's great, as lattes go." He snapped a lid onto his cup and set it down on the counter, then started packing up his tools and crumpling wrappers from the parts he'd used.

The pang of sadness that came over her, watching him prepare to leave, surprised Sage so much it nearly left her speechless. "Thank you for coming out so close to the holiday. Do you have a busy day ahead?"

"Nah." He shook his head while he latched the toolbox closed. "This is my only call. I took today off, but Brevel said it was an emergency, so…" He shrugged, then picked up the toolbox in one hand and the coffee cup in the other. "The service call is free. I won't bill you for the parts since I had them on hand, and it would cost me more time to work up the invoice than they're worth. Call it a Christmas gift."

Sage beamed. "Oh. Well, thank you. It was nice of you to come out."

"I figure I'll stop by the barbershop down the way, get a fresh cut and see what the fellas are talking about."

"Oh, yeah? Mayor was already in here today. He gets a latte every morning during the week and around 11AM on Saturdays. I can practically set my watch by him."

"Sounds like a habit I need to adopt." Bennett gave her a cursory nod and headed toward the door, but stopped when he realized he'd run out of hands. "Could you... uh..."

Sage darted around the counter and crossed the shop in just a few steps. She pulled the door open and watched him walk through, inhaling the faintest scent of an earthy, leathery cologne.

"Thanks again!" she called, standing in the doorway and watching him walk around the back of his truck. He set the box inside the bed and lifted his hand in a wave before heading down the sidewalk toward Guys N Dolls.

Sage never wished she was a guy's gal more in her life. The ones that wore a slinky black dress and four-inch heels to post up at a hotel bar to 'watch the game' and knew what was happening. She was never the type. She let Gordon have his sports on Sundays while she brunched or read, did some knitting or scrapbooking.

She supposed that people changed. And that she couldn't meet someone new by sitting alone watching every episode of *Say Yes to the Dress* and *90Day Fiancé* on the DVR.

But did she *want* to meet someone new? Was she *available*?

Sage whipped around, irritated with herself for even contemplating the question, and stepped back inside the shop, letting the door swing shut. She grabbed a clean white towel from a stack behind the counter and a spray bottle and got busy wiping down the area where Bennet's toolbox had sat. Then she cleaned the machine since it was still dirty from his order.

The front door opened with a swish, but since her back was turned, she called over her shoulder. "Welcome to Roosters! Be with you in a second."

"Take your time," said a deep baritone that was already familiar.

four

. . .

BENNETT

Sage whipped around so fast she dropped the towel she'd been using to detail the espresso machine. Bennett smiled in apology for startling her.

"Hi. Was… is Guys N Dolls closed? They must be slow for Kendrick to close up—"

"No, no. It's hoppin' over there. I just thought…"

He inhaled a deep breath and walked himself through the 3 second version of the speech he'd rehearsed on my way back to the coffee shop. "I guess I figured that if I'm going to the barbershop, I need some place to show off my cut. And I thought maybe you'd want to uh…"

He choked. It had been a while since he'd asked a woman on a date, and he hardly knew what to say anymore. Some of these modern women were bold and did the asking themselves. Bennett guessed he didn't mind that, but he was used to making the moves.

Sage saved him, though. "Bennett Alexander…" She

chuckled, folding the towel over and over again. That's how he could tell she was nervous, too. "Are you asking me out?"

"If… you… want to go out… yes. If not, don't feel like you'll hurt my feelings. It's short notice and tomorrow's a holiday and—"

"I didn't say all that." She dropped the towel on the counter and leaned onto it, her palms flat against the surface. Then she smiled. And he relaxed. "I'd love to. Where are we going? And at what time?"

"Wherever you'd like to go is fine. The rest of my day consists of sitting around a barber shop listening to the young men tell stories about young women so… I can be available whenever."

"I normally close at nine, but it doesn't look like I'm going to get much business today. I'm thinking of cutting out early. Do you feel like Italian? Zucco is good, and they're open tonight. It's a couple of blocks from here."

"Sounds good. Meet me around seven?"

She smiled, nodding. "Yeah. Seven is fine."

"Great." Bennett knocked back the rest of his coffee, which had cooled considerably, and tossed it into the garbage bin on my way out. "See you then."

———

Bennett had dated a few times since Virginia died, but not *dated*. Gone out on a few dates. Not nearly enough, but he wasn't interested in putting notches in a bed post or anything like that. Most dates were something to keep him busy, to get out of the house, or to appease his mother and sister, who felt he should "get back out there". Whatever that meant.

He considered that part — the dating part, the finding a partner part, the sharing his life part of his life to be over. He'd had twenty-five overwhelmingly happy years with one person. The chances that he could find that again seemed slim.

Despite that, Bennett was nervous and excited, anticipating his date with Sage. There wasn't any pressure for her to be his new woman or anything. He just knew it was going to be nice to sit and talk with someone who understood. Not just sympathetic, but *understood* every inch and mile, every nuance of this widow and widower life.

"You gotta go get yourself a nice shirt," said Kendrick, one of the barbers at Guys N' Dolls. "Make a good impression."

"Yeah. All of that," agreed KC, owner of the shop and current mayor of the town of Potter Lake. Bennett was already trying hard not to be an NBA fanboy, but he sucked up advice from the men in the shop, who understood modern dating better than he did, like a dry sponge.

As Kendrick advised, he got a nice cut, then dropped by Ella's Boutique before she closed and picked up a new shirt to wear with some dark jeans. Then he headed home to shower, shave and *get fine*, which is what KC said when he teased him about needing a haircut on Christmas Eve.

No matter how much time he wasted, he was still pacing the living room, expending excited energy until it was time to go.

Bennett finally just sat down on the couch and reached for the remote. Maybe he could catch a game or something to pass the time. The phone buzzed against the wood of the coffee table. These days, Bennett only got calls from work, his mother, or the kids, so it was likely one of them.

It was a photo; the one Rebecca had promised to send. The flowers — carnations and roses and lilies, all Virginia's favorites in a large, beautiful spray sat in front of her headstone. The sight took his breath away and, for a moment, Bennett considered calling Sage to cancel their date, then crawling into bed to stare at the ceiling fan some more.

That wasn't a possibility, though. He couldn't live through

more days where he stared at the ceiling fan. Wasn't that why he had left Charlotte and come to this town? Wasn't that why he was going out with someone? Besides, there was a good chance that Sage would understand this deep mass of heaviness that settled in his chest. Being able to talk to someone about that made him excited again.

Bennett thumbed out a text to Rebecca and Albert, telling them the flowers looked beautiful and thanking them for taking care of the task. He didn't expect a response, since they were probably at his mother's, helping her get ready for the following day. She always cooked like the entire United States Army was coming to dinner.

There would be his sister, Diane, her husband Brandon and their four kids, plus mom's sister Phyllis and *her* husband, Dennis and *their* kids… Bennett was more than a little thankful to not have to endure another year of *so, are you thinking about getting back out there?*

When it was time to go, he hopped up from the couch, turned off all the lights except for a lamp in the living room, and stepped out. He rented the right side of a duplex home. The owner, Monroe, lived on the other side and was almost always outside on the porch. It was a nice space, screened in so it protected him from the elements, facing the street so he could see cars and passersby. And Bennett, leaving his place every day.

Monroe lifted an arm to wave as Bennett descended the steps from the porch, headed to his truck. It was a good thing Sage had already seen the truck, because it would embarrass him if she hadn't. He'd driven the thing around the world a few times, probably, and it was still running. Though it was like a two-ton security blanket, it just barely made the trip from Charlotte and was in desperate need of replacing.

"Merry Christmas to you, Monroe, in case I don't see you!"

"You'll see me, son. Got to come home sometime," he

answered with a laugh. He must have sensed Bennett was in a hurry, because instead of holding him up with random chatter, he just waved and went back to playing checkers against himself.

Bennett drove the few miles to Zucco Italian in downtown Potter Lake, if you could even call it that, pulling into the lot with five minutes to spare. It was a brand new place, with bright lights flashing around a marquee sign, well-manicured bushes and greenery flanking each side of the red brick building.

Sage had already arrived. She was on the phone, pacing the front of the restaurant. Feeling like he was late, even though he wasn't, Bennett hopped out of the truck and locked it, like anyone would want that old, battered thing or any of the junk inside it. He jogged across the half-empty parking lot to the front door.

"Okay, he's here, so I need to go," she almost whispered into the phone. "No, the plan hasn't changed. Let yourself in if I'm not there. Pop the popcorn and start the cocoa going, alright? Alright. See you later, honey. Love you."

"Phone call from the boss?"

She smiled and sighed and slid the phone into the pocket of a stylish little bag. "I shouldn't have even said anything about possibly not being home when she got there. I never have plans, so she had a hundred questions. It's just that… she worries…"

The end of her sentence trailed off, and Bennett was sure she'd be blushing, were her skin not such a deep, cocoa tone. He wasn't the only one who went and "got fine" for the evening. Sage wore a cranberry V-neck form fitting sweater dress with a pair of black leather boots and small silver hoops in her ears. A pendant hung from a chain around her neck, balanced delicately just above the swell of her breasts. Last, she smelled delicious, the heady scent of jasmine and musk wafting over him.

"Well, we're here now." Bennett offered his arm, and she caught the hint, sliding her hand into the crook of his elbow. "Let's put her worry to good use, shall we?"

five

. . .

SAGE

Sage tucked a hand into Bennett's elbow and let him usher her into the restaurant. He looked nice. He wore an obviously new shirt with dark jeans and black boots. He smelled good, too.

She didn't blame Rae for being worried. Hell, *Sage* was worried. As a relatively young widow, unlike her friends, whose marriages had ended in some form or another, she wasn't eager to jump out into the dating pool. A year after Gordon died, her sister had nudged her about trying to date, but Sage couldn't even imagine it. She hadn't even taken off her rings. Rae was even less of a fan of the idea.

"You don't even know this man!" She had protested when Sage called to tell her about the plans that evening. "You know his name and that he works for Brevel. And that's it."

"I know he used to live in Charlotte. He's got two kids, about your age. He's a widower. His wife's name was… Valerie? No, Virginia. Oh!"

Sage snapped her fingers in the air. "Alexander Repair. That's what he said his business name was. He just does work for Brevel. He's not an employee."

"Well, I'm going to check him out," she said.

"What? How?"

"Online. We have his name and his business name, his wife's name. I'll do a background check. Something's got to be out there on him."

Sage had been rifling through the closet for something cute to wear. She didn't exactly want to advertise all the goods... but she wanted to show off a little of the merchandise. She settled on a sweater dress she'd never worn and a pair of boots, then moved through the small apartment while she waited for the hot water pipe to kick in and the bathroom to heat up.

"It's just dinner, Rae! I'm meeting him there. Don't get yourself worked up about it. He's not looking me up on the internet."

"How do you know? Maybe he knows everything about you, and he was just waiting for a chance to come into the shop and started working for Brevel—"

"Did he kill Ned to take his job, then bust into Rooster's and break my espresso machine so I'd have to place a service call?" Sage chuckled, smirking. "You watch too much Criminal Minds. Those writing courses have your imagination working overtime. Are you all packed for tonight?"

Over the years, they had changed the Owens holiday traditions to suit their smaller family, but they still got together on Christmas Eve and spent the evening watching movies, eating popcorn and being thankful to still have each other. The next morning there were presents to open and Christmas dinner to get on the table, carols on the stereo and the Macy's parade on the TV, creating a cacophony of festive sound in the background.

Bennett and Sage were seated in a booth at the rear of the restaurant. The place was dotted with patrons, not busy but not empty, either. The hostess rattled off the specials for the evening and stepped away, leaving them to stare at their menus and nervously eye each other.

Bennett cleared his throat and set down his menu. "I guess we aren't the only people who thought going out on Christmas Eve was a good idea." His eyes bounced around the room, then landed on hers. She noted, just casually, that his eyes were the exact shade of a full glass of rich, dark liquor.

Sage shrugged a shoulder, laying down her menu next to his. "I already know what I'm having. Citrus marinated pork rib roast and their fingerling potatoes with pancetta. I had it last year and I've been dreaming about it for the past three hundred and some days."

"Oh, that sounds good. Virginia could really cook up a good roast. It's been a long time since—" He froze, his eyes growing wide and his mouth dropping open. "I... I'm sorry. I'm rusty at this."

Sage laughed, waving off his apology. "It's fine, Bennett. Really."

"I just... I know you're not supposed to talk about the... you know, the previous—" He sighed, exhaling a loud breath that seemed like it came from the center of his chest. "I was almost ready to back out tonight. Maybe this *was* a mistake. I don't even know what words to say."

Sage reached across the table and laid a hand atop his, giving him a tap to get his attention, to bring his thoughts outside of himself. "You're doing fine. It's alright to talk about Virginia. You'll probably hear some things about Gordon tonight, and I'm not sorry. Don't you be sorry either."

A palpable sense of relief crossed his face. He dropped his shoulders down from around his ears. "Thanks. I'm just... I think I need to stop reading articles about how to date."

Sage laughed. "Probably. It's tough, isn't it?"

"Especially the second time around. Do this, say that. Don't do this *or* that." He blew out a breath, shaking his head, then reached for the glass of water the waitress set in front of him.

Sage ordered her roast and potatoes, and he ordered the creamy chicken marsala. They split a bottle of wine since it was a special occasion. The waitress bounced away to place the orders and bring the wine.

"So…" Bennett toyed with the white napkin folded neatly next to his silverware. "How many dates have you been on since Gordon died?"

"I could count them on one hand. It's not fun. Especially since the men I meet don't seem to be half the man Gordon was. Uh… present company excepted."

Bennett smiled, almost laughing. "I was worried for a second. But I agree. I lost a good thing and I'm not gunning to replace her. But I want companionship, and that's been hard to find. They don't make them like Virginia anymore." He smiled, bringing his eyes to hers. "Present company excepted."

It took a few minutes, but by the time the salad bowls came and went and then dinner plates hit the table, they were chatting like old friends.

"Rebecca is one of those people that's just good with numbers," Bennett was saying. "She got her undergrad degree in Finance; she's finishing up her master's soon. She's gunning to be the youngest VP ever promoted. She's a Commercial Account Manager right now, though."

Sage hummed appreciatively, chewing a mouthful of succulent pork roast before commenting. "Sounds like she has a good head on her shoulders. Maybe she should open her own bank. Wouldn't hurt to have another black bank owner."

"True," he agreed, nodding. His plate was nearly clean, having sopped up the vodka sauce from his Chicken Marsala with a hunk of crusty Italian loaf. "That's definitely on the career plan. First, she wants to conquer Bank of Charlotte. Their masthead is all old white men. She wants to break that glass ceiling. And I don't blame her."

"Same with Rae. She's in a writing program… uh, Writing for Television and Stage, I think it's called. Eventually, she'd like to direct. She's creative, I'll give her that. I hope it translates into work that pays bills, you know? In my day, that was stuff you did in your free time. You went to school for something that paid real money."

"Aw, I wouldn't worry too much. Look at all these black women writers and directors out there. Oprah, Ava DuVernay, Regina King… what's her name, from the Cosby show?"

"Oh, Cousin Pam! I know who you mean; I can't remember her name, but she's always Cousin Pam to me."

"Yep, and Issa Rae… hell, even Viola Davis is writing and directing, not to mention the ones we never hear about, the up-and-coming writers. There'll be plenty of space for her when she's ready. And, like Rebecca, she might want to break down some walls herself."

"I guess that's a good way to think about it. So, what about your son?"

Bennett sighed, pushing his plate away. He balanced his elbows on the edge of the table and clasped his hands under his chin. The crease in his forehead deepened and his eyebrows drew together.

"Albert is… The boy is smart, but he's like Teflon. Nothing sticks. He's on his third major, with no graduation date in sight. He's okay with numbers, but thought he might be more artistic, so he was an Art major. But he didn't want to take art history classes. Then he discovered that he enjoys cooking, so he applied to the Charlotte Culinary Institute. They asked him to wait a year and reapply. Well, he lost interest in that. So…"

He shrugged his shoulders dramatically. "Instead of

paying for him to flop around another year, I suggested he take some time off and decide what he wants to do with his life."

Bennett reached for his goblet and tipped a swallow of the lush red wine into his mouth. "That was two years ago. I'm not pushing, though. He's working at the home improvement store, and he seems to like it there." He held his hands up in surrender pose. "All I want is for him to be happy, to pay his own rent and car insurance. He's managing that."

Sage couldn't keep her laughter at bay any longer but tried to at least cover her mouth with her hand as she giggled loudly. "Youth is wasted on the young, I heard once. I guess that's all you can ask for, though. Weren't you nervous about leaving him back in Charlotte?"

"Nah," he answered, sipping more wine, then swishing it around in his glass. "He's a kid of many talents. He's intelligent. Lands on his feet. I think he's afraid of getting stuck somewhere. He wants to love what he does. Maybe he... I don't know. Maybe he looks at me and thinks he doesn't want to be that guy. Fixing things for a living. It's nothing prestigious, but it kept us in good living."

"But you like what you do. Right?"

He shrugged. "Not always. I fell into the repair business when I got laid off of a job. I had a natural curiosity about how things work, and as a boy I had to be the one to get things going round the house. It was just my mother and me and my younger sister. I bet he remembers the lean years of Alexander Repair, and Virginia working overtime at her sales job to make ends meet. It cut into our family time. We all had to make sacrifices."

"Now that, I understand," Sage mused, commiserating. "There were a lot of years that Rae wasn't wearing name brand clothes and shoes while we built Gordon's business. We made it, though. And he left us well taken care of."

"What did he do?"

"Oh, he was like your daughter. Into numbers. He was a Financial Planner, CPA, Business Manager, all of that. He worked for a firm for a long time but decided that he wanted to strike out on his own. I still wanted a little freedom to help, but still do my thing, so I worked at my sister's cafe."

"So that's how you know so much about running a coffee shop."

"Yeah. When Rae got accepted at Healy, she talked me into doing what I said I always wanted to do. My sister's shop is also named Rooster's. We consider my shop to be sort of a franchise."

"Looks like things are going well in that department. What about... other departments?"

Sage knew what he was asking, but was so amused she couldn't resist playing with him. "Are you being fresh with me, Mr. Alexander?"

The corner of his mouth tipped up when he laughed. That made her laugh, too. "Too soon?"

"Actually... not at all. It's been five long years, you know."

"About that for me, too. I uh... I miss it."

"Especially this time of year. Gordon loved most holidays, but Halloween and Christmas, he really went all out."

Bennett swirled the wine in his glass and sipped. "Yeah. Christmas was Virginia's favorite, too. Mostly because uh..."

Sage sat through the pause that followed, giving him the time he seemed to need. He swallowed what must have been an enormous lump, and when his eyes rose to hers, they were glassy.

"Sorry," he mumbled, his voice low and gravelly. "Anyway, you said Gordon was really into Christmas?"

"Yeah. And then you said Virginia loved it too. Because..." When he didn't respond, she reached across the table and curled her fingers around his. "Bennett, it's okay. I get it. Talking helps. Go ahead."

He heaved a loud sigh, one that must have emptied his chest of air. Then he sucked a breath in, and said, "Today is… her birthday."

"Oh…" She whispered. "I am so sorry. What a hard day for you and I'm over here rambling—"

"No, no. It's good. The rambling. It's just that we usually set aside today as a family to celebrate her. You know, not lump her in with Christmas. She…" He nodded, licking his lips. "Yeah, she really liked that. And then she made an enormous deal out of Christmas. The food and the trees and the lights and the perfect gifts. I couldn't replicate that. It just became a burden to try. But I miss it."

Sage's eyes slipped closed, and she nodded, humming in commiseration. "My daughter wanted to hold on to our old traditions. I do it for her, mostly. But it's not the same." She paused, giving the moment it's time to pass, and then softly added, "I'm sorry you're without her now. Especially on her birthday."

"Thanks," he answered quickly, gulping the last of his wine. He pushed the goblet away and reached for the still full glass of water, swallowing half of it in a few seconds. "Think I'd better start hydrating. I'm a lightweight, lately. So uh… let's change the subject. What do you like to do for yourself? You know… away from the shop?"

Sage brightened. "Oh, I used to have all kinds of hobbies back in Ocala. I haven't picked any of them back up. I like a good Stitch & Bitch. And I used to be a pretty good bowler—"

"Okay!" Bennett sat up, beaming across the table. "I haven't picked up a ball in a while, but I'm a passable bowler."

"Oh, yeah? We should… well, if you want to bowl sometime, Lake Lanes just renovated. I heard it's real nice in there. It's next to the Kit Kat. You ever been out there?"

"Once or twice. I hear it was a rough place back in the day, but since the new Mayor took over, it's mellowed out some.

Bowling sounds like fun, though. You have your own ball and everything?"

Sage frowned, reaching for the last of the bottle of wine. "What real bowler doesn't have their own ball?"

six

. . .

BENNETT

The evening was mild, the air cool with the breeze off of the lake but not cold as they strolled from the front door of Zucco to Sage's car, a late model Toyota. She groaned, cradling her midsection.

"I'm so full, I don't know how I'm supposed to eat the junk Rae and I planned to eat tonight."

"Pace yourself," Bennett replied, a hint of amusement riding his tone. He shoved his hands in his pockets, though he wanted to drop an arm around Sage's shoulders. He didn't want to alarm her, however.

She seemed comfortable with him, though, threading her arm through his as they walked across the empty parking lot. They'd shut the place down. In fact, they'd sat in the warm corner of the restaurant so long that the manager had to lure them outside with a gift certificate for $20 off of their next visit.

It surprised both that the hour was so late. Time had flown by so fast once they'd started talking about hobbies; bowling

— hers and fishing — his. They'd each promised to treat the other to their favorite activity in the coming weeks.

Sage had wisely parked near a streetlamp. They neared her car and stood beside the driver's side door. The glow around her lit her up like the aura of an angel.

"Well…" Bennett began, his hands still in his pockets.

"Well…" Sage answered, smiling up at him and breathing a light sigh. "This was fun."

"I agree. Any time I can eat myself silly is a good time."

"Then you'll have a lot of good times around Potter Lake. I uh… I was so surprised when you came back to the shop. I guess I figured… I don't know… I didn't think you were interested."

"I'm surprised I came back, too. Not for the reason you're surprised, though. I was interested the moment I saw you. And even more so when I learned you were a widow. There's a special understanding between us."

"There really is," Sage agreed.

"And I wanted to say thanks for that. Maybe that's what I've been doing wrong all along. Looking for everything else when I needed to be looking for a connection with someone. A spark. So… thanks for being the spark."

"Well, you're welcome. No one's ever called me a spark before. Sassy, spirited, smart mouthed, yes. Spark is a new one."

"I like that I could give you something new. And uh…" Bennett moved in, a few steps closer. They were so close, he could feel the heat and smell the perfume wafting from her skin. "There's something else I'd like to give you. If that's okay with you."

"Oh, it's fi—"

Sage never finished the word, because Bennett's mouth pressed against hers, so hard her lips smashed against her teeth. She whimpered, ever so slightly. Bennett broke off the kiss and stepped back.

"I'm... wow. That was..." He couldn't help but laugh. "That was so *thirteen-year-old boy's first kiss.* I'm... I know what I'm doing. I promise. It's just—"

"It's okay," Sage soothed. "I'm rusty, too. Just relax. Come here." She opened her arms and reached for him. He stumbled forward, feeling silly and slightly tipsy. "Pull your hands from your pockets first. Now slide them around my waist... there you go."

Sage stepped in, closer and closer still, her arms resting on his broad shoulders. "You remember how this goes," she whispered, tipping her face up to his. In the moonlight, and the bright glow of the streetlamp, she was just about the most beautiful woman he'd ever laid eyes on. His arms tightened around her, pulling her in even closer, molding her body against his.

Bennett dipped his head to meet her, and this time, the kiss was airy, soft. Sage moaned and opened her mouth, her tongue flicking out to tease the seam of his lips. By instinct, he opened. Their tongues met and he couldn't stop the groan that rolled up from the pit of his belly. His hands began to roam, his palms exploring a few inches above her waist.

When his hands dipped below her waist and cupped the generous roundness there, Sage sucked in a breath and pulled back from the kiss, pulling her arms from around his neck. With rapid pants of ragged breath, her eyes darted around the parking lot for a few seconds.

"I'm sorry. I didn't mean to make you uncomf—"

"No!" Sage barked, holding up a hand. "Don't apologize. I... I was having a great time. It's just that we're..." She gestured toward the Zucco marquee, still lit by what seemed like a million fluorescent bulbs. "If I didn't have my kid waiting at home for me..."

Bennett grinned, oddly proud of himself. He'd taken a few steps that had him shaking in his boots before. "Then I hope this won't be the last time we see each other. You're supposed to let me win a game or two of bowling—"

"And you're supposed to teach me to fish."

"Right. And... I'd very much like to see where kisses like that end up."

"Me too," Sage answered, her palm over her chest and her voice a little breathy. "I... have to go. Rae is probably about ready to call the FBI, I'm sure. But I definitely look forward to seeing you again."

"For sure. Is the shop open after Christmas?"

Sage smiled. "Bright and early, 6AM."

Bennett nodded, then turned to head toward his truck. "See you then, Sage. Goodnight."

"Goodnight, Bennett."

seven

. . .

BENNET

"Got a lil' pep in your step, brother!"

Monroe waved from his perch, a glass of something amber in one hand, a cigar in the other. Bennett had parked the pickup in front of the house and walked up the sidewalk toward his half of the duplex. He hadn't noticed a lift, but then again, he was distracted by thoughts of that kiss with Sage.

Bennett detoured from the planned path to his front door and climbed the few steps to Monroe's porch. He had propped the screen door wide open, so Bennett stepped in and sank into a weathered but comfortable leather chair covered by a faded afghan.

Without asking, Monroe pulled a glass from a cubby next to a small, dorm sized refrigerator. A collection of liquor bottles sat on top of it, some full, some nearly empty. Monroe picked one out, twisted off the cap and poured a few splashes into the bottom of the glass and slid it over.

Bennett took the glass and the cigar offered. After clipping the end and lighting up, basking in the smoky, woodsy aroma, he downed a sip of whiskey.

Monroe leaned back, glass in hand again. "I heard down at the barbershop you was takin' Ms. Sage out on a date. Y'all have a good time?"

Surprised, Bennett's brows shot up toward his hairline. "Man, news travels fast around these parts."

"Yeah, you'll learn that pretty quickly. Hard to keep yourself to yourself. Well? How was it?"

"It was nice. She wanted to go to Zucco, that Italian spot?"

"Aw yeah. Nice place, if you like red sauce and such. Ms. Sage doin' alright?"

Bennett nodded, puffing more of the cigar, sipping more whiskey. "She's good. We talked about... you know, her husband. Her daughter. The shop. Nothing too deep."

"Suppose you two have a lot to talk about, what with being in the same situation. My Gladys been gone about fifteen years now."

"Oh. I'm... I'm sorry to hear that."

"I ain't." Monroe wheezed a long laugh. "She ain't dead. Just gone. Run off with one of my so-called friends after the mill shut down and jobs dried up. Ol' ungrateful...."

Bennett tried not to laugh but couldn't keep the chuckles down. "You're somethin' else, Monroe."

"That I am. Heard that a time or two. Hell, if I was twenty years younger, I would have asked Ms. Sage out myself. But... she don't want an old man. Now, a young buck like you, though? I saw it when I first laid eyes on you."

"Saw what, sir?"

"Just... you. The way you are. I knew you wouldn't be chasing after some of the young ones that have been moving out here. You'd want someone... seasoned. You know what I'm saying? Lived some life. Got a good head on her shoulders. Thought to myself, he'd make a great match for that coffee shop lady."

Monroe stopped to sip more from his glass and take a few puffs from his cigar. "Real nice night," he commented, gazing out over the yard and the homes across the street. "So you had a good time, you say? You'll be seeing her again?"

"Yes, sir," said Bennett, sighing into his glass. He knocked back the last of the whiskey and stamped the cigar out. "I'd better head on home. My kids and my mother will be calling early to make sure I'm alright."

"Well, go on ahead then. If you get lonesome, I'll be here. There's a big Christmas Dinner at Helen's Kitchen at five o'clock. I'm heading over there around four to help set up tables. Could use a few extra hands."

Bennett nodded. He'd been trying so hard to make it through Christmas Eve that he hadn't even thought about plans for Christmas Day. Doing some work, keeping busy? And having some of Helen's famous cooking? Couldn't pass that up.

"Yeah. Sounds good. I'll see you tomorrow, then."

After a handshake and a nod to Monroe, a walk down the steps, across the sidewalk to his own steps, Bennett unlocked his door and stepped inside the house. It was dark, save the single lit lamp in the living room. That was a Virginia thing. She hated coming home to a dark house. He'd taken on the habit, even now that she was gone.

He turned off the lamp, then headed to his bedroom at the back of the house, unbuttoning and discarding clothes and shoes as he went. His mind naturally drifted to thoughts of Sage.

Sage in that dress.

Sage up against him.

Sage's perfume, the softness of her lips, the sound of her laughter, the way a smirk made her lips purse and twist to one side...

Sage... *not in that dress...*

Bennett groaned, first sitting, then laying back across the

bed. He stared at the ceiling fan, as he had done every morning and every evening since moving to Potter Lake. But tonight… his thoughts weren't on his wife, his love, his peace. He rolled to his side, trying to tamp down the pangs of guilt that wracked him.

Because no matter how hard he tried, he couldn't *stop* thinking about Sage.

eight

. . .

"Look, Rae… I didn't die. He didn't turn out to be an unsurp, or whatever you call it—"

"Un sub!" She screeched, pacing the tiny, tiny space that was my kitchen. "Unknown subject!"

"Girl, if you don't settle down with that screeching and these dramatics." Sage frowned, her eyebrows drawn close together. She reached for the silver ladle and a thick mug. "This cocoa is ready. Grab those mini marshmallows."

"Why won't you tell me about your date?"

"Because you take everything too far and out of context. I'm not giving you ammunition to look him up. He's fine." She poured two ladles of creamy milk chocolate into a mug and handed it to Rae, then picked up the second mug. "I mean… really *fine,* if you must know."

"I do not need to hear the lustful moanings of a forty-five-year-old. Especially when she's my mother."

"I thought you wanted to hear about my date?"

"I do. I do not, however, want to discuss his fineness, when it's related to my mother."

"You're no fun. Come on." She picked up both mugs, which Rae had topped with mini marshmallows, and headed to the living room, a few steps away. "What are we watching first? Home Alone?"

"We're not watching anything until you put on the pj's I brought for you." Rae plopped down on the couch and stretched her legs out to prop her feet, clad in festive Christmas socks, on the coffee table. The rest of her was covered in a pair of all-in-one pajamas, also festive for the season. Hers was an image of a decorated Christmas tree.

"I'm not putting that thing on," Sage grumbled. "Sitting around here looking like Frosty the Snowman in a Christmas onesie. No."

"*Mooooooooom-uuuhhhhh...*" Rae whined. "You promised. Go put it on. You can change when you go to bed!"

"I don't—"

"Ma! Do it!" Rae barked, pointing toward the bedroom.

Sage stared stubbornly at the TV. Then huffed and cut her eyes at her daughter. Then punched her fists in the couch to help her stand and stomped toward her bedroom. "I don't know when you got to be so bossy, but I don't like it."

"I've been bossy my whole life!" Rae called from the living room.

Sage really didn't want to put the thing on, but had to admit, the longer she stared at the screen print image of a happy snowman, all laid out on the bed, the cuter it seemed. *Well... just for a few hours, I guess.* As she peeled off the t-shirt and leggings, her eye caught the pile of clothing she'd worn on her date. The boots stood in the middle of the room; the dress was puddled around it, since she'd changed as soon as she walked in the door.

She smiled to herself, thinking about Bennett. Those eyes, man. *Those eyes.* And those shoulders made him easy to hold on to. That chest was so nice to be up against. And his lips… after the first kiss, of course.

Sage chuckled to herself, stepping into the fleece garment, pulling it up around her waist, then pushing her arms into it. He must have been so nervous, poor guy. But she'd been able to get him to relax. And that second kiss? Her skin flushed and a wave of heat radiated through her at the memory.

She was ready for more of that.

"Stop stalling!" Rae shouted. "Let's go! We've got movies to watch!"

"We're only watching two movies, lil' girl." Sage snapped the last button closed and stepped out of the bedroom. "You're not keeping me up until dawn."

"Not my fault you was out kissing boys at all hours of the night."

"Uhm, excuse me?" She settled on the couch, tucking her legs up under her. She cradled the mug of chocolate in her lap. "Mr. Bennett Alexander is a *man*, thank you so much."

Rae shot up a hand, turning her face away. "Okay, that's enough. I don't need to know any more about his man-ness."

"See, you start stuff and don't want to finish." Sage giggled, then reached for the remote. "Let's do Home Alone, first. Hand me that popcorn, girl."

———

They'd spent the evening watching and laughing at silly 7-year-old Kevin McCallister foiling a home robbery, eating an entire bowl of popcorn and finishing the cocoa. Sage stretched and yawned, dragging the nails of one hand through her short, messy bob.

"I know I said two movies tonight, but I really am beat. It was a long day. How about we fire up the second one after breakfast?"

Her gesture must have been contagious, because Rae

opened her mouth and roared a satisfying yawn herself. "Yeah, I'm beat. Tomorrow it is. Are we still doing Helen's Kitchen for dinner? Last year was bomb."

The first few years in Potter Lake, Sage had tried to cook and serve a full Christmas meal, but there just wasn't the room or the equipment. The previous year, Helen and her husband Orlando, owners of Helen's Kitchen, Potter Lake's finest home cooked soul food restaurant, opened up their restaurant for a special dinner. Tickets went fast, but Sage snagged a couple for them. Dinner was amazing — they'd talked about it for days — and a new holiday tradition was born.

"Bomb is good?" When Rae glared at her, she shrugged. "Yeah, that's the plan. Are you going to be okay out here on the couch? You want to get in the bed with me?"

Rae was already unfolding blankets and fluffing pillows. She reached into the duffel she'd brought with her and grabbed a small cloth bag. "No, I do not want to share that little ass bed with you. I learned my lesson the first year. But let me brush my teeth and put my scarf on before you get in there."

"Alright. Just don't leave a mess."

"Not enough room for a mess," Rae grumbled, passing her on the way to the only bathroom in the apartment, off of the bedroom. Sage followed her, picking up the path of clothing on the floor and on the bed as she went.

"So your date -ent -ell?" Rae asked, muffled through a mouth of toothpaste. She poked her head around the bathroom door and thrashed the toothbrush around in her mouth.

"Rae Ann, I know I've told you about that! Getting toothpaste spit everywhere. Get in the bathroom and brush your teeth." Sage moved to stand in the doorway behind Rae. "And yes. The date went well. Very well. I'm going to see him again."

Rae straightened. Sage watched her eyes, cognac brown like her dad's, grow big and round in the mirror. She reached for a silk scarf that she kept bunched in the small bag and unfurled it, then wrapped it around her hair, capturing her two-strand twists in the fabric.

"Like… seeing him when he comes into the shop? Or… *seeing* him?"

"A little in between. He's supposed to take me fishing. We'll probably go bowling. I haven't touched a ball in—"

"Mom!" Rae whipped around, the small bag in hand. "Bowling was a… you and Daddy thing!"

Sage paused, then pushed away from the entryway and re-entered her bedroom. Rae followed, her brows knit together, making it obvious she wasn't pleased.

"Yes. Yes, it was. Though we didn't do so much of it the last few years—"

"Well, Daddy got busy with the business, and you didn't want to go to bowling league by yourself. So you're just going to replace Daddy and start bowling again?"

"Rae, I'm not—"

"I mean, what else are you going to have him do that Daddy used to — you know what? Don't answer that. Good-night, mom." Rae brushed past her, bumping her shoulder as she went.

"Rae… Rae! Honey…" But Rae had determined she was done listening. She was already under the covers on the couch. She flopped to her side, presenting her back to Sage, and pulled the blanket up over her head.

"Goodnight," she whispered, reaching up under the lamp-shade to douse the light in the room, then tiptoed to her bedroom and pushed the door closed.

Then heaved a long, loud, emotion-filled sigh.

All she had wanted was to ease that dull ache in her chest that was ever present. Every moment of every day for the last nearly six years, it was there. For a few hours with Bennett, it hadn't been there.

She ached for it to disappear again.

nine

· · ·

SAGE

Sage sipped on a mug of coffee, steam still rising from the rim. In the small kitchen, Rae sullenly went through the motions of chopping onions and scallions, then mixing eggs for their traditional Christmas breakfast of crustless quiche and bacon. Sage tossed a salad and made the sweet, mustard-based dressing that she knew Rae loved. Brunch was a quiet affair, full of one-word answers, mumbles, and shoulder shrugs.

Rae's mood disintegrated into the afternoon. She was so glum during the viewing of *The Santa Claus* that Sage reached for the remote and paused the playback. Rae was on the loveseat, opposite her on the couch, her feet hanging over the edge of the armrest. She was still in her holiday onesie, though the festive spirit that they were supposed to encourage was nowhere near the room.

"What?" Rae asked. "I was watching."

"We should talk about last night. Our conversation ended poorly. Let's try it again."

Rae sighed, swinging her legs down to the carpeted floor and reaching for her duffel. "Nothing to talk about. I guess it's been long enough. You're replacing Daddy. I mean…" She pulled out a tube of lip balm and popped the top, then aggressively rubbed the cherry scented wax across her lips. "You're getting older. You don't want to go into your twilight years alone. Makes sense that you'd be looking for some—"

"Rae Ann Owens!" Sage's sharp tone jabbed into the atmosphere, making her daughter jump. Slowly, she lowered the tube of lip balm and recapped it. "I have never raised a hand to you, but if you don't find a muzzle for that mouth right now, I might start. I've had enough!"

"Look, mom, I just—"

"I said be quiet!" When Rae had closed her mouth again, albeit with a frown, Sage continued. "I've put up with a lot over the last few years and listened while you expressed your opinions about everything from the shade of my lipstick to the size of the cups I use at Rooster's. You've been here for me since Daddy died, holding me up, making me move out here, making sure I'm okay. And I appreciate that. I really do."

Sage got up, then walked across the room and sat next to Rae, dropping an arm around her shoulder. She expected Rae to stiffen, but instead her shoulders slumped, and she leaned into the side hug.

"And you're damned right," she continued softly, "I'm getting older and no, I don't want to go into my twilight years — which are quite a way off, by the way— alone. But in no way am I trying to replace your Daddy. And nobody in this town is going to be able to. Am I being understood?"

"Yes ma'am," Rae mumbled, her head bowed in appropriate contrition. "I'm sorry. I'm just… having a hard time with you wanting to do stuff you used to do with Daddy."

"If you're having a hard time, think about what I'm going through. This is an entirely new ball game. I'm doing the best I can to still live and enjoy my life. Nobody's picking out

China patterns. It's a few dates, a good time. I need your support, here, Rae."

"Okay, Mom. I'm here. I just… I don't want to hear stuff about how *fine* he is. Just, you know, keep telling me he's nice to you. That's all I need to know."

"You've got a deal. I'll call my sister to dish about how good he smells and those big shoulders of his and—"

Rae rolled her eyes and groaned, "*Mooooom.* That's exactly what I mean."

Sage laughed, then laughed again. "You are still no fun! So is it okay if I pick up bowling again and maybe take my new friend with me? Even though it's something I used to do with Daddy?"

Rae was quiet, her head bowed so low that her chin nearly rested on her chest. After a few moments, her chin lifted, and she shrugged. "I guess. But you better not be letting him win."

"Another deal. Now, there's a bunch of presents under that tree with your name on them." She nodded her head toward the small, pre-lit tree that Rae had loaded down with too many ornaments. "You know we have to send pictures of you opening Grandma's gift, so we'd better get on it. Then I'll shower and get dressed. I want to get to Helen's early, so we don't have to stand in a long line."

ten

. . .

The last person he expected to see that day was Sage.

He supposed it was because her daughter was in town, but he pictured her sitting cozy and warm at home with a plate full of delectable goodies in front of her, maybe something cheery blaring on a TV in the distance. So when he marched through the space at Helen's kitchen, gripping a six-foot table in each hand, he ground to a halt so quickly that Monroe almost crashed into him.

"Let's move, brother! Running late," he heard from Monroe behind him, carting chairs for the tables he was carrying. In seconds, he was on the move again, setting up the tables and pushing the chairs underneath.

Helen came behind him, floating a mistletoe patterned cloth over each table. A bright smile lit up her entire face when she stepped back to survey the room and saw Sage in the doorway, with a young woman who couldn't be anyone but her daughter. She was a younger version of Sage to a tee. Same almond-shaped eyes, same thick lips, same pointy chin, same brown skinned complexion.

Both were casual in leggings, over the knee boots and long sweaters. Tiny snowmen dangled from Sage's ears and her daughter wore candy canes.

"Sage!" Helen squealed. "And Rae! Good to see y'all again this year!" She crossed the room in a few steps and grabbed each of them, pulling them into the hug that seemed inevitable if she was in the room. Helen had even hugged Bennett, after telling him he was a big glass of chocolate milk.

"We're still setting up. You're welcome to pitch in. I need napkins and plastic ware at each seat, I need beverages set out… oh, Sage, you can help me get the coffee on! This year I have a crumb cake for dessert, and it goes well with a nice Colombian blend."

Helen, Sage, and her daughter disappeared into the kitchen, chatting amongst themselves. Bennett realized he'd been staring at Sage the entire time.

And she'd been stealing long glances right back.

Monroe was behind him, hauling more chairs into the room. "Boy, if you don't close your mouth, a fly gonna get into it. Come on, now. I'm ready to eat and we can't sit down until we set this room up. Let's go."

Snapping back into action, Bennett and Monroe headed toward the storage shed behind the restaurant to pull out more tables and chairs.

———

Helen's Kitchen was packed wall to wall with people. Every table and chair were occupied, and some stood around the edge of the room balancing a plate on one hand and a fork in the other. The Temptations holiday album was on full blast and the whole place held the scent of roast turkey, prime rib, potatoes, greens, yams, and fresh baked rolls.

As promised, Helen's crumb cake and vanilla ice cream

topped off the meal perfectly. Sage manned the beverage station, handing out bottles of water, ladling up spiced cider or freshly brewed coffee. Bennett, stuffed to the gills, ambled across the room where he'd been sitting with Monroe and a few of his friends.

"Sage," he greeted her, with an upward head nod.

"Bennett." She graced him with a smile that warmed his belly. "I didn't expect to see you here."

"I didn't know I was coming until last night. My neighbor Monroe invited me."

She brightened, almost laughing. "He is hilarious. Always coming into Rooster's flirting."

Bennett smiled. "He mentioned that. So you're saying I have competition?"

"A lot, if all you're talking about is flirting. The old men in this town love a pretty lady."

Bennett laughed. "I'ma tell Monroe you called him an old man. So uh…" He nodded toward the industrial sized coffee maker. "Is this a Rooster's blend?"

Sage shook her head. "Just something Helen orders in bulk. It's good. It's not Rooster's, but it's good. You want a cup?"

He nodded. "Only if you think you can break to join me."

"I suppose people can press this button and pour a cup of coffee for themselves for a few minutes." Sage poured two cups of coffee, then doctored hers with cream and sugar. Bennett did the same, then led the way to the front door of the building.

They stepped outside, where it was not warm, but not cold. Helen and her husband, Orlando, had decorated the facade of the restaurant and the surrounding trees and bushes with Christmas decorations. The bench that sat outside the building was also strung with a few lights. Bennett lowered himself to the bench and scooted over, making room for Sage.

She settled in next to him, her hands wrapped around the paper cup for warmth.

"You suppose this town gets snow, ever?" Bennett asked.

Sage shook her head. "Hardly ever, from what I hear. A little too far south. Maybe if a freak storm blows through Alabama."

"Oh. Would be pretty if it did. Especially around the lake."

"Mmhmmm." Sage sipped her coffee, then sighed as she swallowed. "So, you want to talk about the weather some more, or did you have a reason for asking me out here?"

"I..." Bennett chuckled. "I really didn't have a reason. I saw you come in earlier, while we were setting up. I didn't get a chance to say hi, so I'm doing that right now. You uh... you look nice."

He was sure she was blushing, even if it was on the inside. The edges of her mouth tipped up in a smile and her lashes fluttered. "Thank you, Bennett. Not looking so bad, yourself."

He had rolled out of bed after tossing and turning most of the night, around noon, and felt like he'd dressed in a fog. It was still difficult to wake up without Virginia setting the house up for the day with music and turning the Christmas lights on, the scent of cinnamon rolls and coffee in the air.

He showered, then pulled on a pair of jeans and a sweater the kids had sent him, a navy blue V-neck alpaca wool sweater. He wore a white collared shirt under it and absent-mindedly splashed on some aftershave before sliding his feet into a pair of loafers and walking out the door.

"Thanks. A gift from my kids. They know what Dad likes. Those earrings..." He paused, pointing at them. His lips twitched in an effort to not laugh. "Were those a gift?"

She fingered the dangling snowmen and smirked. "Rae knows what Mom likes. But still buys this silly stuff and makes me wear it. We're lucky that it would be inappropriate for me to wear the snowman onesie she made me wear last night."

Bennett laughed, then lifted his cup to his lips. "Wish I could have seen that, actually," he said, then tipped the brew into his mouth.

"Yeah, well. If I have it my way, I will bury it at the bottom of a drawer. Maybe I can lose it until next year."

He laughed again, then leaned forward, resting his elbows on his knees. "She's beautiful. Looks just like you. She sounds spirited, like her mama."

"Oh, so much like her mama. But if you would have met Gordon, she looks just as much like him. Acts like him, too."

"Oh yeah?"

"He was a pushy man. Opinionated, too." Sage chuckled softly, then grew quiet. Her eyes dropped to the cup of coffee in her hands. Bennett sat back, then lifted an arm and dropped it to the bench behind her. He gripped her shoulder and gave her a reassuring squeeze.

"You good?" He asked quietly.

Sage lifted and lowered a shoulder. "Rae and I fought last night."

"Fought?"

"Well… argued…. about my date. About you, about…" She sighed, lifting her eyes to the view of an overgrown field marked for sale and shimmering in the distance, Potter Lake.

"About me?"

"Sort of about you. We talked it out this morning, but the more I think about it, the more I see her point. She feels like I'm trying to replace Gordon. And maybe she isn't all the way wrong about that."

"Do *you* feel you're trying to replace Gordon?"

Sage didn't answer for a long, long moment. Then she stood. "I don't really know. And until I do, maybe it's best to just keep to myself for a little while longer. I'd better get back inside. Rae will look for me."

Bennett didn't even get a chance to argue before she

turned on a heel and marched back up the sidewalk toward the restaurant. She flung the door open and stomped inside, the door falling closed behind her with a slam.

"Well," he said to himself. "Messed that up without even trying,"

eleven

. . .

SAGE

For the second time that week, Bennett surprised her. After she had that emotional tantrum at Helen's and stomped out, she wouldn't have been surprised if she'd never seen him again.

"I was just… a fool, Rae," she'd ranted that night. After dinner, they took a walk around the west end of town to look at the Christmas displays and exercise off a bit of three-helping dinner. "Just acting stupid. He probably thinks I'm crazy."

"He doesn't think you're crazy, mom."

"How do you know? You wouldn't even meet him, with your stuck-up self."

"I didn't meet him because he's new to your life and he shouldn't be meeting your children this early." Rae gave Sage an impatient glare, then hooked her arm around her mother's and picked up the pace of their steps. "Anyway, I'm sure he doesn't think you're crazy. Just… call him and explain that you're just scared, and this is a big move for you and—"

"I can't call him. I don't have his number. I only have the number to Brevel, and I'm not calling them to get his number. I just have to wait to see him and believe me... this is a small town, but if you want to avoid someone, you can."

Sage remembered having a long, hilarious conversation with Leslie Baker-Cavanaugh over mocha frappes on a rainy Sunday evening. She'd talked about knowing that Kade had moved back to Potter Lake and successfully avoiding him for over a year. She knew the second she saw him that she'd fall right back in love with him, and that was the last thing she wanted.

Or so she thought. Within months, they'd moved in together, were married and pregnant and making everyone absolutely sick with their sweet love story. Truth be told, Sage had held to that story ever since. Gordon was the love of her life... but who said you couldn't have more than one?

Her next love was waiting. She was sure of it.

"Mom," Rae drolled, leading her back to the car. They'd made a full loop and were reasonably tired enough to go back home and resume their holiday movie watching before Rae returned to her apartment the next day. "He doesn't think you're crazy. You did say you needed some time or whatever, so... if he gives it to you, take it. But..."

She paused at the passenger side door, then grabbed Sage's hands and squeezed them. "I may not have met him, but I watched him watching you. I've seen that look on a man's face before. Daddy had it. There's no way he can resist you. So you just keep being Sage Owens and he'll come around."

And here he was. All six feet and then some, big shoulders, wide chest, friendly smile, and deep, sexy laugh of him.

Here. He. Was. And Sage couldn't think of a single thing to say.

"So, how much coffee do you drink in a day?" He asked.

She settled into the booth across from him, her own cup of

coffee in front of her. "Depends on the day. And the season. In the summer, I drink a lot of iced coffee, iced tea. In the winter, I drink more hot tea than coffee, but some days just… call for coffee. I try to balance it with water."

Silence befell them both. Sage sipped and Bennett sipped, but neither seemed bothered by the quiet.

"So… since you fix all manner of electronic things, do you find that you collect them?"

Bennett laughed, tossing his head back. "You been talking to Virginia? I used to have a warehouse full of stuff, and she'd bug me all the time about my junk. Can't figure out how to fix it if you never broke it, especially the vintage stuff. But then it became cheaper to buy an updated model than to repair the older one, so people stopped bringing a lot of those items in.

"I had to cull my collection when I sold the house. I still have a fair amount of things in storage back in Charlotte. Once I get into another house, I'll find a way to display some things I just like having."

Sage nodded. She loved to hear him talk, the way the bass in his voice almost made the table rumble. But also, that he wasn't a gruff, loud man. There was a lot to like about Bennett Alexander.

"I wanted to apologize," Sage blurted. Bennett's brows met, his forehead wrinkling in apparent confusion. "I… the other night, I was having a sort of… a…"

She huffed, nearly out of breath for no real reason, except that the words she wanted to say wouldn't come. Maybe this just wasn't the right time, in the middle of their workday with customers halfway listening and the time clock ticking. A wonderful idea crossed her mind.

"You know what? I'd like to have you for dinner. Over… for dinner," she corrected, giggling. Bennett laughed. "Let me try that again. Would you like to come to dinner tonight? My place. Nothing special, but I'd love to relax and talk. Alone."

"Don't get me wrong, I'd love to be dinner."

"See, there you go, getting fresh with me."

"You started it." After a moment, he gave her a single head nod. "I'll bring the wine."

———

Sage bumbled around her apartment, fluffing pillows, and adjusting curtains in between checking on the pot on the two-burner stove. It was much less of a kitchen than she was used to, but she was learning to make it work. The vegetables were in a double boiler on the stove, but the Instant Pot she'd recently purchased had the chicken and wild rice ready in a flash.

By the time three loud, loud knocks sounded at the door, she was a bag of nerves. A pretty bag, though, in a thigh length, deep v, scalloped neck bodycon dress that clung where appropriate and had the split up the leg that left nothing to the imagination. Since she was at home, she finished the look with a pair of slippers... but they were her good ones, the fluffy black pair with the faux fur.

When she opened the door to let Bennett in, Sage was nearly bowled over, first by the very scent of him; a subtle minty, green tea, flower scent that was light but suited him, then the fitted t-shirt, jeans, and dark sneakers that he'd traded for his daily uniform.

"Hi," she finally uttered, after staring for longer than a few seconds. She stepped back so he could enter the apartment, amused that he had to duck to get inside.

"Hi, yourself," he said, handing her a bottle that he fisted by the neck. He made no secret of the fact that he was taking her in, head to toe. And she was enjoying it. He handed her the bottle, saying. "I wasn't sure what we were having, but this is a favorite."

"A Sauvignon Blanc, great choice!"

She took his jacket and hung it in the hall closet. "Well, this is pretty much it," she said, waving her arm around the living room. From the front door, the kitchen, the dining room and the living room were visible. "Back there, around the corner, kind of, is my bedroom. And the bathroom if you need it."

"This is a cute place," he mused, nodding, and looking around. "Good construction. Just enough."

"Yeah, I like it. Though, like you, I have a collection of things in storage back in Ocala. Just waiting to need a place big enough to put them somewhere. Maybe when Rae is out of school, but she's talking about moving to LA or New York when she graduates."

She'd been talking while she worked, dishing up plates of chicken and rice, adding a few spears of steamed broccolini and a roll to the side. "We can eat in the living room. Make yourself comfortable."

They sat on the couch, side by side, plates perched on their knees and ate, talked and laughed through *Best Man Holiday*.

"You know how I know Terrence Howard is a good actor?" Sage asked, as the credits rolled. She picked up Bennett's plate and carted it to the kitchen with her own.

"You can't hardly stand the dude, but you have to see every movie he's in?"

"Exactly!" Sage squealed, pointing at Bennett, who had made himself comfortable, stretching an arm long the back of the couch, removing his shoes and crossing his socked feet under the coffee table. "That's exactly it. I wouldn't share air with that man, but he sure knows how to bring a character to life."

"Maybe we heap our feelings about the characters he portrays onto the man?"

"No, I don't think so. I think he's an ass." Bennett

laughed, which made Sage laugh too. "Hey, you want some ice cream? It's that no sugar added stuff. I heard you at the shop, when you said you couldn't really handle the sugar in cookies."

"Yeah, a scoop will do me."

Sage brought two small bowls, each holding a scoop of vanilla bean ice cream, to the couch. She sat next to Bennett, but closer than she'd sat for dinner.

"Do you have diabetes?"

"Nope," he replied, licking the cold cream off of his spoon. "Just old. Ever since about 40, I can't hold my liquor and sugar gives me all kinds of problems."

Sage chuckled, scraping the bowl with the edge of her spoon. "You aren't old. The kids say *seasoned*. I like that."

"That sounds good. Seasoned, then."

He finished the bowl and slid it on to the table. Sage's bowl joined his a few moments later. When she moved to get up to take them to the kitchen, he landed a hand on the smooth dark skin of her thigh, exposed by the split in the dress.

"Don't get up yet. Relax. You said you wanted to talk, earlier. What about?"

"Oh..." Sage tugged at the dress to pull it down some. It had ridden high on her hips and her entire leg was hanging out of it. But then... in a moment of sheer determination to step outside of herself and do things she wouldn't normally do... she left it.

And laid a hand on top of Bennett's. He turned his hand over, palm up. She slid her palm across his and let him close his big hand around hers.

A shiver coursed through her, though she wasn't cold. Just... *aware*. Aware that she was in her apartment, alone with Bennett Alexander, a man who had occupied her thoughts since the moment she saw him.

"The other night..." She shook her head. "I guess I was

just too deep inside my head. Day to day, I don't really know what's happening. Some days I still feel married, like I could roll over and he should be right there. Some days I just know that I know that I know that he's gone. I feel so empty and so lonely.

"I get that way around the holidays. Then Rae and I fought over whether I was trying to replace her father, and I thought I was fine, but those words just kept circling my head. Like buzzards. Like a record on repeat. I mean…"

She shifted, moving, so she faced him, could see him more easily. "Bennett, I… I like you. And I know we don't know each other, but I like what I know. And I'm… seasoned, too, so I'm no dummy. I know that feeling is mutual. And… I just got scared. Terrified."

"Of… what, though? It's not like I proposed, or anything."

"That's exactly what I told Rae," Sage answered, laughing. "But then, I guess I didn't listen to myself. I got hung up on missing Gordon and wanting someone to be with and I felt like it wouldn't be fair to you if that's all it was."

"Sage… listen. If something pops off between us, I'm all good about it. If all it ever is, is some fun for you and me? It's worth it. I miss Virginia. I miss sex and kissing and having somebody to hold on to, somebody to give tight hugs to, somebody to take to dinner, to spend time with. Am I trying to replace my wife? No… not in so many words."

"But it's not unrealistic to think that's what's happening."

"Sure. And I don't know about you, but I'm dealing with a lot of guilt over that. But I like you more than I feel guilty about liking you. I want to spend time with you more than I feel guilty about wanting to spend time with someone new."

Sage nodded, understanding his dilemma completely because she was in the same spot herself. "I feel better, knowing I'm not alone, here."

"Good. You know what would make me feel better?"

Sage smiled, knowing what was coming, but asked anyway, "what would make you feel better?"

Bennett leaned over until his lips were so close to hers, she could feel his breath on her skin. She closed the distance, tipping her head up so her lips pressed into his in a gentle kiss. He pulled back, then went in again, this time with parted lips and a breathy sigh, capturing her tongue as it flicked out to meet his.

Sage sucked in a long breath through her nose, then heard the pleasured moan before realizing it was actually her. Bennett chuckled, mid kiss, then hummed *mmmhmm* before moving in closer and deepening the kiss.

Before Sage realized it, she was on her back. Bennett hovered, dusting her skin with his lips from her chin to her neck, down her chest, tracing the path of the scallop neck, down one side and back up. He tasted the glowing skin of her breasts, lingering there for the most amazing few minutes of her life, recently.

"Oh… God… Bennett."

He hummed but didn't stop. He kept exploring until his teeth found the tight pearl of her nipple through the dress and her thin, lacy bra. He nipped it lightly, over and over. With each nip, a spark shot through Sage, pushing out a whimper that grew in volume until she couldn't take one. more. second of teasing.

She gripped the collar of the dress and pulled it back to reveal the simple, black lace bra, then freed herself from the bra and, without even thinking about how she should be demure and tease him and not give in too easily or too early, she grabbed Bennett's chin and pulled him down to her, guiding his warm mouth and wet tongue to close over the bud and rasp over her nipple. Over. and over. And… over.

Familiar waves of arousal washed over her, making her drunk and heady with desire, with want. She wanted Bennett in every way possible. He had relaxed, settling between her legs, moaning as he licked and sucked, circling first one nipple, then after freeing the other, doing the same. She was pulsing, head to toe, but especially at her core. Her body bucked and writhe under his, and when his hips hunched into her, she yelped at feeling the thick lump.

"Bennett!" She gasped, pushing up onto her elbows. "Wait!"

twelve

. . .

BENNETT

Bennett hadn't seen Sage in days. That had been on purpose.

He wasn't sure what he'd said to turn her off, or that he'd said anything to turn her off, for that matter. She had mentioned keeping to herself for a while, though, and he wanted to give her the space she needed.

But he missed her. And he knew it was odd to miss someone he'd just met, had no actual relationship with, and had turned tail and run away from him as soon as the opportunity to get close had arisen… but he missed her.

"Give her a few days," Monroe had advised. "She's probably gun shy, you know? She said it had been a while. You're in the same boat, so you understand, I'm sure."

"Yeah," he'd answered. "I get that. So, I'll give it time."

But now he was sitting in the parking lot outside of Rooster's, watching her patrons walk in, heads down against the gusty winds that had blown in over the past few days, then walk out with smiles and tall cups of Rooster's brew. He fought with himself, trying to decide if he should go in, or drive away like he'd done every time he pulled into the parking lot without seeing her or speaking to her.

Today he had to go in. He was eager to see her, to say hello to her. Besides, he had an hour before his next service call and he could use a cup of coffee. Before he could change his mind, he turned the key in the ignition and popped the latch on the driver's side door. He stepped out of the truck, slid his key ring into his front pocket, and walked across the parking lot.

At the door to the shop, he paused. Sage and another employee were at the front counter. A few tables were occupied, but there was no one at the front counter. He couldn't hear the conversation, but Sage and the employee were having what seemed to be a spirited, laugh-filled conversation, full of hand gestures and sassy neck rolls.

He stepped inside the shop, at once enveloped by warmth and the scent of roasted coffee. Whatever conversation Sage was having, it died as soon as he stepped in. She stood stock still, her eyes wide but a hint of a smile on her lips. At least she didn't frown. Maybe she was happy to see him.

Her employee smiled and centered herself at the counter. "Welcome to Rooster's! What can I pour for ya?" She chirped.

Bennett smiled at her and approached the counter. Though he'd rather order from Sage, he wouldn't be so rude as to demand it. "Just a cup of coffee, please. Dark roast. Large."

"Sure thing. Would you like a sugar cookie or two? Mayor's mama in law made them fresh this morning!"

He shook his head, digging out his wallet and pulling out a crisp bill. "Can't really handle the sugar. Thanks, though." He slid the bill across the counter. She rang up the order and gave him his change.

Sage grabbed a cup and poured his coffee, then tipped her

head toward the end of the counter. Bennett slid the change into his pocket and gave the clerk a smile and a nod, then met Sage a few steps away.

"Hey there," he lobbed quietly, while adding cream and sugar substitute to his coffee, then stirring it until it lightened to a tempting, lovely, dark beige color. "Good to see you."

"Good to see you, too," she said, leaning onto the counter, her hands clasped together. She wore her standard Rooster's t-shirt and jeans, but her hair seemed to be silkier, bouncier. And… shorter? It had an extra flair to it. "You're staring at my hair. You like it? I had Evonne over at *Curl & Dye* give me a cut and a nice press and curl. She said she hates doing press and curls. I told her not to be so good at it, then 'cause that's all I'm ever going to ask her to do.

"It looks nice on you. I like it a lot. So…" He gulped his coffee, then regretted doing that because it was still hot. "How uh… how've you been?"

"I've been fine, Bennett. And you? Haven't seen you around for a few days. Thought you'd forgotten about me."

"I'm good. You did say you were going to keep to yourself for a while. Was trying to respect that — was I supposed to ignore that?"

"I guess not." Her gaze dropped to the counter, making her eyelashes sweep against chiseled, high cheekbones. Then her eyes flicked up to his. "It's just that I was going to call you. To… talk. But I had no way to reach you…"

"Oh." He reached into his pocket to pull out his wallet again and slipped a card out from the thin stack he kept there. "Now you have my card. That's my mobile number. Call anytime."

She took the card and stared at it like it held military secrets, then tucked it into the pocket of her jeans. "So… I can take a break. I mean… I'd like to talk to you. If you want to—"

"Want to?" He laughed, almost too loudly. "Woman, you haven't seen me sitting outside this place every day, wondering if I should come in here? Hell yeah, I want to. I'll go find a seat."

68

thirteen

. . .

BENNETT

Bennett was as surprised as he imagined she was to find himself laying on top of her, her skin marked with evidence of his enjoyment. When she sat up, uttering a strangled cry in his ear, he panicked.

Bennett lifted his head, freezing all motion. "Do you need to stop? What's wrong?"

Sage pushed against his shoulder, forcing him up. "I don't want to stop. I don't have plans to, anyway… but if you do, we need to upright, on opposite ends of the couch, because…"

She shook her head slowly, a grin creeping across her lips. "Like I said, it's been six years. I'm way past ready."

Relieved, Bennett sat up. "I don't want you to think I planned on this. Or that I expected it."

"But I did," Sage replied. She swung her legs from the couch and stood, grabbing his hand and pulling him up. "Come on. Let's get where we can relax."

Sage's bedroom was… small could be a word. Miniature

would be a better fit. The bed was a full size because that's all that would fit in the room. A five-drawer chest stood against one wall and the other was, Bennett assumed, a closet, the kind with the doors that slid to one side or the other. He guessed as well that the closed door led to the bathroom.

What the room lacked in size, it made up for in character and decoration, with a purple-pink theme. Blown glass vases with silk flowers bearing all shades of purple, photo frames in deep eggplant and bright fuchsia, and matching bedspread and curtains in royal purple with gold pinstripe woven through it.

"It's not much to look at—" she said, but Bennett stopped her, pausing her with a finger to her lips. Then he replaced his finger with his own lips and kissed her. When he pulled back, he was cradling her face in his palms.

"I have no complaints about this room. It's very… you." He kissed her again and stepped back. "Where do you want me?"

Bennett thought he heard 'all over me' but he wasn't sure. Sage muffled it, pulling her dress up and over her head. She tossed it to the corner nearest the closet and disposed of the wispy black lace bra the same way. He pulled his t-shirt up, but Sage cried out for him to stop.

"You're opening my present, man. What's wrong with you?"

A sultry laugh rolled from her throat as she tugged on the hem of his t-shirt and slowly slid it up, revealing a taut belly and molded chest. So he wasn't a cover model with a six pack and pectorals that danced all by themselves. He was, by every definition, a beautiful man.

"Okay, this can come off. Arms up." He lifted his arms and grabbed the shirt to help her pull it off. "Put it anywhere. You won't need it for a while." Then she reached for the band of his jeans, nimble fingers loosening his belt and then the top button, then slowly tugged down the zipper… so slowly he thought he might lose his mind, or at the least wave her fingers away and rip the zipper down himself.

She pushed his jeans down his thighs; he kicked first one leg and then the other until they pooled at his ankles. He stepped out of them, then used his foot to push them behind him, where he'd dropped his shirt. Now he stood in her bedroom in just his briefs.

"Come sit," she said, directing him to the edge of the bed. As soon as he sat, Sage climbed onto him, straddling him and sitting on his lap. His hands cupped her fully exposed breasts. Her nipples were hard, aching for his fingers. Or his mouth.

She moved a breast towards him and fed a nipple into his mouth. He sucked on it greedily as she moaned softly, her hips beginning to grind against him. As he sucked one breast, he fondled the other, flicking the nipple, causing peals of pleasured sounds and more forceful writhing. He switched from one to the other, making sure they both got the attention they deserved.

In a swift move, Sage pushed his shoulders, so he was laying back on the bed. To match her sudden moves, Bennett grabbed her by the waist and pulled her down, rolling on top of her. "I think we're both still overdressed."

"Don't have to tell me twice!" Sage bucked her hips up and so she could pull the thin boy shorts down her legs. Bennett did the same, writhing out of his briefs, then sinking back into place. Sage was warm and soft, but solid, beneath him. He liked this, feeling her skin to skin. And sensing the heat that was coming from her body.

He rolled to his side and reached out to smooth a hand down her thigh, then back up the inside, toward the warmth. Sage's legs opened a little wider to make room for his exploration. The first touch was light, barely there. Sage gasped and tensed, and when Bennett pulled back, she reached down to lay a hand over his. "Don't stop. I'm just... the anticipation..."

Bennett could understand that full well. He was almost, but not quite painfully erect and anticipated some reciprocal touching and stroking, but first he wanted Sage to be comfortable with him. So he took his time, rubbing and teasing her, in awe of how wet he could make her just by touching and kissing her.

They were both a sweaty, panting mess, but the feeling of being intimate again was so intoxicating, he didn't dare stop. When Sage reached for him, wrapping her hand around him and beginning to stroke him, he thought his eyes might roll back into his head. It had been... years since anyone else touched him. Five years, nine months, and twenty-four days, to be exact.

He released a loud grunt into the air, and his hips bucked with the rhythm of her movements. "Sage... I—it's been a long time. I might not—"

"Shhh," she hissed, cutting him off with a kiss. She gripped his shoulders then and pulled him so he was between her legs again. His body was sending out signals like morse code, searching for her heat, her warmth, something to sink into. Once again, she gripped him, but this time it was to guide him to her.

"I'm ready, if you are. I want all of you, Bennett... please."

That whimper, that tone of pleading in her voice did him in. He positioned himself and pushed into her, almost filling her with a single stroke. He pulled back and plunged again. And again. And... *oh God*, again and again and again.

fourteen

. . .

SAGE

"Yes, fuck me, Bennett!"

Shit. Did that just come out of her mouth?

She suspected so, because Bennett chuckled, then grabbed her legs, hooking his arms behind her knees so she was wide open. He hovered above her, bucking his hips, using his whole body to bring her the most pleasure she'd experienced in… well, ever.

Gordon was a perfect lover, but that was just it. He was tidy, liked to tick off boxes. Licking? Check. Sucking? Check. Petting? Check. The old thrust-thrust-thrust move to the slow grind, back to the thrust- thrust-thrust until he brought it home? Check. For twenty-three years, that was how it had been, and since she'd never been with anyone but Gordon, she thought that was how it was supposed to be.

Until Gordon died. And one of her friends gave her a pornographic movie as a gag gift. And when she finally got up the nerve to watch it, she became… *curious* about how other men made love. Had sex. Did the do.

Bennett was satisfying every curiosity. And then some. He liked to vary in length and depth. He liked to pepper her with kisses in between strong, satisfying strokes. And the sounds he made? She gushed at the thought.

"You good?" He asked, his face mere inches from hers. She stretched up to kiss him, starting a dance with his tongue that she felt the pit of belly, which just made her grind into him harder, meeting him plunge for plunge.

"I'm real good right now, Bennett. Don't stop, never stop…"

"Gotta stop sometime, baby girl. I promise you'll be worn out when we do, though."

At that moment, to her surprise, Bennett pulled out. She started to sit up, propped on her elbows. "What happ — *ohhhhh.*"

She fell back again at the sensation of his tongue rasping over her clit, then taking it into his mouth to suck on it, then more nipping and licking until she was climbing the walls, grunting and yelping in indescribable pleasure.

This… *this* was something Gordon rarely did for her. Maybe on special occasions he would venture south, but rarely. She'd never known any different, but now that she had? Holy fuck. She clung to his head, holding him between her thighs while she writhed against him. Then it was so much… too much…

Her climax hit hard. And loud. She ground herself against his mouth, eking out every bit of her first orgasm that wasn't self-induced in six years.

"That was amazing to watch," said Bennett, kissing his way back up her body. "You're beautiful when you come. Ready for more?"

"Hell yeah," she answered, right before he entered her again, picking up his long, hard, pounding strokes. "Fuck-ing… *shit!* I'm gonna come again!"

"Do that shit," he said, exertion showing on his face. "I'll go when you go."

Sage found that… sexy. And not just sexy, but sensual. He was getting off by watching her get off. And get off, she was. She wrapped her arms around his torso and bucked her hips into him, grinding her clit on his pubic bone. The most delicious sounds and parts of words and phrases were uttered through clenched teeth, grunted into her ear.

Bennett worked with the strength of ten men; Sage was deliriously on edge… and then fell over the cliff of a body stiffening, convulsive, explosive orgasm, apparently taking Bennett with her, from the loud grunts and the *shitshitshitshit-shit* he grunted into the air.

He collapsed, as if his legs had just given out. He heaved breaths, sucking in air, his body coated in sweat. In a few minutes, it seemed, he gathered the strength to lift his head, find her lips and kiss her. Not a wild, passionate kiss, but an acknowledgement of what they'd just shared.

"That was… so incredible." Sage reached for a pillow from the head of the bed and tucked it under her neck.

"Yeah?" Bennett said. His voice was raspy, like his throat was dry. "And to think… that was just the first time, when you run into all the snags and kinks. Next time, it'll be better."

Sage paused. "Next time? There'll be a next time?"

Bennett's head lifted from his resting place on her chest, between her breasts. "You're gonna give me just one taste of Sage Owens and then cut me off?"

"I wouldn't dream of doing that to you," she said with a giggle. "I just… was hoping it wasn't weird for you. You know, to not be with Virginia."

Bennett paused, as if to contemplate that. "I don't think weird is the word. Just… different. How about you?"

Sage nodded, deciding not to list all the ways that Bennett rocked her world better than Gordon ever had. "Different, yeah. And I welcome different any day that ends in Y and twice on Sunday."

Bennett laughed, then with great effort, rolled to the right and sat up.

"You're not leaving yet, are you?"

He glanced back at her, where she was splayed out on the bed in post coitus delirium. "You want me to stay?"

"A few minutes and a bottle of water and I could be in the mood for more of that different you're offering."

fifteen

. . .

SAGE

"Whatever you did with her hair last time? She wants that again." Rae, the director of not only Sage's life but everyone else's, chatted with Evonne at the *Curl & Dye* at her chair. Sage's hair had been washed and Evonne was gently rubbing a cotton towel over her head.

Evonne laughed, then got to work on what had become Sage's signature hairdo: a flirty, bouncy neck length bob with a side bang. "Rae, how's school going for you over at Healy this year? And you know I'm not talkin' about your classes. Your mom keeps me up on all of that. I'm looking for the *good good.*"

"She's not gonna tell you nothin' with her mama sittin' right there!" Tamera called from her chair.

"I don't have any secrets from my mom," said Rae, dropping into the empty salon chair next to Tamera's station. Leslie spent three days a week at City Hall, helping her husband run Potter Lake. The other days, she was at her station at the Curl & Dye. Today, she was downtown, making sure the annual New Year's Eve fireworks show and block party went off without a hitch. Sage was in charge of the coffee and hot chocolate, so she'd come in early for her hair appointment.

"Well, spill the juice then," said Evonne, pumping creme into her hands, then slowly working it through Sage's hair.

"My classes are good; they're all really fun this semester. But I know you're looking for information on my new boyfriend."

With dramatic flair, Rae paced the shop, regaling the two stylists and the only other customer with details. Sordid, raunchy, *extensive* details about the biology major she had been seeing for the past few months. The young man had, apparently, made an impression on Rae.

In the mirror, Sage watched Evonne's facial expressions change with every revelation. "You can say all that of that with your mom in the room?"

"I've heard it all, and much more," Sage offered, frowning. "At least she's telling someone else for a change. Every text, every look, every love note. If he farts in her direction, I get a phone call. I can't talk about *my* man, but I have to hear about hers every day. I'm tired, and I'm not even in this relationship."

"I told you, it's weird to hear about my mom getting down and dirty. I don't want to think about… old people… bumping together…" Rae shivered, over-dramatically so.

"Rae Ann, go find something to do!" Sage yelled, trying not to laugh. "Go on! Get out of this shop! Take the car, go get some lunch. Get out of my face."

Rae grabbed her purse by the long strap, slung it across her body and marched out of the door, cackling all the way. When the laughter inside the shop died down, Sage sighed, wiping tears from under each eye.

"That girl is a trip and a half," said Evonne. "But now that she's gone, we can talk about your man. Bennett was in here a few weeks ago, working on a couple of the dryers. I admit, I had my eye on him, but he was real quiet."

"She was about the break the dryers again, just to have him come back," said Tamera, blow dryer in one hand, round brush in the other. She flipped the dryer on low and pulled the brush through her client's hair at the nape, resulting in silky strands. "Should have just gone over to Rooster's."

"He can be quiet, I guess. He's a thinker. But if you get him started, like ask him about something to do with electronics, and he'll talk your ear off."

"That is *not* what I want him to talk off, Sage. But I'll be respectful, since he's your man and all."

Tamera pointed the nose of her blow dryer across the room. "Evonne, I'm about to kick you out of this shop! Behave!"

"A lady doesn't kiss and tell," said Sage. Evonne had rolled her hair and covered it with a cap. The next step was to sit under a medium heat for a half hour. "But between you, me and the curling iron… he can talk some panties off, too!"

"Ms. Sage, you're a mess! Just a mess! Get on over to those dryers!"

sixteen

. . .

BENNETT

Bennett regretted saying he'd work for the day. When he'd agreed to work New Year's Eve, he wasn't dating someone. Now instead of being available to help Sage set up her coffee and hot chocolate station for the New Year's Eve Block Party and Fireworks show, he was driving all over Potter Lake and Healy, making repairs on everything from washers and dryers to heat pumps, not to mention his Brevel customer list, who'd all seemed to break their espresso machines on the same day.

At least he'd kept busy most of the day; it made the day go faster, bringing him closer to when he could clock out, head home, and get ready for the evening. Sage was bringing Rae for snacks and drinks. Then they had to head downtown for the holiday festivities.

His phone buzzed in his pocket, and this time he wasn't sure who'd be calling. Sage made good use of his mobile number, and his children, mother and sister still called as often as they always did. He pulled out the device and smiled at the display.

"Hi ladybug! Happy New Year, almost. How're you doing?"

"Hi Daddy! I'm good, just checking on you."

Rebecca's voice came through so clearly, he could hear the exact vocal intonations that made her sound exactly like her mother. Sometimes it made his heart sink; he longed to hear Virginia's voice again. Today, though, it brought a skip to his heartbeat and a lift to his mood. He was turning another corner, another year. He was making it.

"I'm doing just fine. Really, this time," He added with a laugh. She'd know what he meant. "Got a full day today. Everybody broke everything."

Rebecca laughed, another sound that brought him joy and memories of Virginia. "It's good that you're busy. Do you have plans tonight?"

Bennett told Rebecca and Albert about Sage a few days ago. They took it better than he'd thought they would, even asking a few questions about her. "As long as you're happy, dad," Albert had said. When he assured them that he was, indeed, happy, they seemed happy for him. His mother had been overjoyed to hear he'd gotten back out there and had met someone nice, who understood what he was going through.

"Yeah, the town does a big deal every New Year's Eve. My uh… Sage is working a table, so I'm going to help her out and we'll watch the fireworks. Should be nice."

"Good, Dad. Good. I'm happy you won't be sitting at home by yourself."

"Thanks for being concerned, ladybug. Hey, love you, but I'm coming up on my next call. I don't want to be late. I'll talk to you and Albert soon, alright?"

He disconnected the call and slid the phone away, then hung a right into the parking lot of *Bubble Up Laundromat*. A dryer was on the fritz, and the place was unusually busy, so he'd scheduled a last-minute service call to take a look.

The scent of laundry detergent and bleach hit him in waves as he walked through the double doors to the front counter. "Good afternoon, I'm Bennett Alexander from Alexander Repair. Here to check out a busted dryer." He flashed his ID badge and slid a business card across the counter to a young male clerk wearing a paper hat that read Happy New Year.

"Oh yeah. It's the one over in the corner on the left. People love that one, because it's bigger than the others. Last night there was actually a line to use it."

"Okay. And what's it doing… or not doing."

"It's taking forever to dry anything. I checked the lint filter… nothing seems wrong with it, but it's just not heating up. There's nothing like warm, wet underwear, you know what I mean?"

Bennett laughed, hitched up his tool belt and headed to the broken dryer. A half hour and a repair to a loose heating coil later, the dryer was up and running, pumping out hot air.

"Thank you so much!" The clerk beamed. Having all your appliances working must be so satisfying. "My regulars will be so happy!"

"Happy New Year to you," Bennett said, handing him the invoice. "Call me if anything else goes wrong. This is due in ten days."

"No problem, Bennett! Happy New Year to you!"

After giving the clerk and the patrons a nod, Bennett left the shop and heaved a sigh of relief. He peeled off his zip up hoodie with the Alexander Repair logo on it.

He was officially finished with calls. He had plans with his lady for the evening. And he was about to walk into a New Year the happiest he'd been in a long time.

———

"Two hot chocolates, large!" Sage called over her shoulder. Behind her, Rae and Bennett were working the line. This was the second year that Sage was in charge of the hot beverage station and her popularity, Bennett had heard, had grown exponentially. The line, which had been full all evening, was thinning out since the fireworks were starting soon.

And now they were serving none other than Mayor Kade Cavanaugh and his wife Leslie. She balanced a tiny replica of KC on her hip. Bleary-eyed but happy, Kade Junior gave Sage a big smile and babbled something in baby language.

"Happy New Year to y'all," Bennett said, handing them each a tall hot chocolate, garnished with whipped cream.

"Happy New Year," KC replied, his hand out. He and Bennett performed the complicated handshake that had been developed at the shop, a series of taps and twists and grips.

"I don't know who made up that silly handshake, but they need to retire it," Leslie said.

"They take all day to shake hands," Sage teased, grinning at Leslie, and making faces at KJ. He responded with gusts of laughter.

"He's delirious. He took a long nap, but this is way past his bedtime." Leslie jostled him on her hip, then KC took him and set him up on his shoulder. "The fireworks are about to start, so you can close up anytime."

"Looks like you're my last customers, so we'll close up."

"Okay. Thanks for doing this again, Sage. We really appreciate it."

"Anything for the Mayor and his wife. Y'all have a great time, then get that baby in the bed!"

"Will do! See you at Rooster's tomorrow, I'm sure." Leslie waved, then jogged to catch up with her husband and son.

Sage watched them walk away, her arms folded across her chest. Bennett heard her sigh. He slung an arm over her shoulders, then squeezed her to him. "You good?"

Sage tipped her face up to him. "I'm good. Why?"

"Heard that sigh. Just checking."

"Aw… it was a happy sigh." She turned to him and wrapped her arms around his waist. He closed the circle around her with his other arm, pulling her up against him. He dipped his head, resting his forehead on hers. "You good?" She asked.

"Baby… I'm not just good. I'm great. Thankful for you and that broken espresso machine. Let's go watch the mayor try not to set this town on fire and get our New Year's Eve midnight kissin' on."

"Think I could get a preview?"

"Oh, let me get ghost before the smooching starts," Rae drolled from behind them. She smiled, though, as she walked past them, following the crowd to the fireworks display.

"Good, she's gone. Now I can kiss you like I want to."

"Are you getting fresh with me, Bennett Alexander?"

His lips met hers and lingered there for a few sweet moments before he pulled back. They exchanged a long, meaningful gaze. And then a smile.

"I am most definitely getting fresh, Sage Owens. I hope to keep getting fresh with you all year long."

"Well alright, Mr. Bennett Alexander." Sage tipped her face up to him for another kiss. "I'd best let you get to work."

———

Want to be the first to know what's happening in Potter Lake? Join the Newsletter!

enjoy a sneak peak of book 3 in the potter lake series

"evonne busted into taj's life like a wrecking ball!"

Quiet, reserved musician and Registered Nurse Taj Wright has his world turned upside down when he rents his guest house to Evonne, a spunky hair stylist who's a big fan of murder podcasts. The attraction between them at first sight is immediately electric. When a storm ravages Potter Lake, and they're forced to share close quarters, they can no longer resist each other.

But... now what? Evonne is on a mission to prove that she isn't the screwup that was sent home from Spelman College ten years ago. Taj is floundering, trying to tamp down a desire that can't be stifled. The last thing either of them wants is an emotional attachment to a temporary relationship.. but does it have to stay temporary?

On a rainy night in Georgia, two hearts meet. They're never the same again. Grab this fun and funny small town Black romance.

evonne

Not that I was afraid because I was no punk, but the salon was scary at night.

Especially tonight, when storm clouds dampened the brightness of the moon, and the wind howled around the corners, pelting the plate glass windows with rain. The shadows had a way of playing tricks on me. A crash of thunder shook the strip mall that held The Curl & Dye, and I couldn't help it… I yelped.

I couldn't *wait* to get out of there.

I'd already rushed my last customer out, tying a spare scarf over her fresh hairdo and standing in the open doorway to make sure she got into her car. Then I pulled the double doors shut, flipped the OPEN sign to CLOSED, and locked myself in. A bolt of lightning ripped a seam in the inky dark sky. Seconds later, another sonic boom of thunder sent me running to the back room.

"If you had already moved out here, you wouldn't be too far from home right now."

I grabbed a few cleaning supplies from the closet and left them near the door, then started my evening ritual of poking a soft-bristled broom under each salon chair and gathering flyaway hairs that had escaped Leslie and Tamera's quick cleanup.

"Now you have to worry about driving back to Healy in this downpour."

I clicked my tongue, frustrated by my habit of procrastinating. I had more than enough saved to get a place in Potter Lake, a move I'd been putting off ever since I was hired full time at the salon. Two years ago, Potter Lake was a struggling town with nothing much to offer but a bunch of olden days shops and even older townspeople.

Then we got a new young mayor, and overnight, Potter Lake transformed into a mini-metropolis that prided itself on being a big little town. Mayor Cavanaugh was doing good things, establishing conveniences, and encouraging folks to set down roots and be a part of the community. New residents meant an increase in clientele, and between Leslie's salon and Kade's barbershop, there was no excuse to be walking around town with your hair looking like *'who did it and why'd they leave it that way'* as my Grandma Bobbie would phrase it.

Moving out to Potter Lake would make my life much more comfortable and far quieter, but I kept putting it off. Another month of inconvenience meant another few bucks in the bank. I could put up with my family for a month. Then the month would roll by, and I'd talk myself into another. Then another... and before I knew it, I was six months past my deadline and sick of screaming at my sister, Ebony, to pick up her half of our room.

"It's time just to do it," I declared, running a soft cotton towel over the appliances at my station. I was making good money at the shop, and sponsorship opportunities for my web channel, *Hair by E*, were starting to roll in.

And my parents finally seemed to not be angry anymore about that unfortunate incident that landed my ass back at home, ten years ago.

I wiped down every chair in the salon, using the orange scented leather cleaner that Leslie liked, cleaned out the shampoo bowl and refilled the pumps from the industrial sized storage containers. Leslie had already taken the day's deposit to the bank, so I tucked the evening's receipts in a locked drawer, checked my station for anything out of place, and pulled my jacket, which wasn't going to anything for me, off of its hook.

"I'm wearing this new wig, too. I'm about to be looking like a drowned rat."

I stepped outside and pulled the doors shut behind me, twisting the key into the lock as I went. I pulled the jacket up over my head, inhaled a sharp breath, and darted out into the pounding rain. The heel of my booties click-clacked against the uneven, pocked pavement as I made a mad dash for my car in the corner of the parking lot.

"And that's another thing…"

I sped into a jog as I neared my car. Key fob in hand, I fumbled with it to find the unlock button so I could get in.

"If you had yourself a man, you could have joined Leslie and Tamera for date night, but *Nah*. You have to be the hero and volunteer to work late so they can Netflix and chill. And what do you get out of it? Noth—"

The toe of one shoe caught a divot in the pavement, knocking me off balance. I flew forward, arms flailing before I thought to stick out at least one hand to break my fall. I hit the ground heavily and slid a few inches.

"Woo, *shit!*" I felt that in a major way, all the way up my arm.

I moaned in pain, pulling myself up on all fours, then tried to get my feet under me so I could stand. My jacket was no longer protecting my brand new wig, a sleek platinum blonde lace front, from the elements. Instead, it had landed in a pothole. Thankfully my bag ended up on top of it. I grabbed it by the handles and groped for the keys I had dropped.

And that's when I saw the blood.

I almost fainted, staring wide mouthed at the gash down the side of my palm to my wrist. Dark red rivulets mixed with rain and oozed down my arm, gathering at my elbow. Without thinking, I yanked the scarf from around my neck and wrapped it around my hand, then grabbed my keys, unlocked the car, and lurched for the driver's side door handle.

As soon as I fell into the car and dumped my bag on the passenger seat, I slammed the door against the torrents of rain. My arm was beginning to throb, the pain gaining a sharp edge to it. Blood seeped through the thin, emerald green silk scarf I'd worn to match my sweater.

Using my good hand, I dug through my purse to find my phone and dialed the first number that popped up— Tamera. "Shit!" I hissed when it went straight to voicemail. Same with Leslie. Then I remembered that Kade and Leslie, Erik and Tamera, and Kendrick and Monica were at the opening night festivities of the new Cineplex, one of those theaters where you could eat, drink and watch a movie. All of their phones would be off until the movie was over.

I selected the next number I could think of and prayed while it rang. Just when I thought it would roll over to voice-mail, the line picked up.

"Hullo?" A sleepy male voice answered.

"Romey!" I sat up, adding pep to my voice. "Hey, handsome. You in bed already?"

"Nah, I'm on the couch. Just tired. What you up to? You tryna come through? You need a teddy bear to comfort you through this storm, huh?"

I rolled my eyes but threw in a flirty giggle. "Mmm, maybe… I need a favor first."

"Unnh," he grunted, then made sounds like he was shifting positions. "I don't get paid 'til next week, so if you askin' for cash—"

"One time, I asked you for ten dollars, and now you act like I ask you for money all the time. Nobody wants your call center paycheck."

He grunted, sucking his teeth. "Vonne, what do you want? I'm tired."

"I'm stuck in Potter Lake. I fell in the parking lot and hurt myself; it's an open cut and bleeding bad—"

"So go to the hospital. What do you need me for?"

"Potter Lake doesn't have emergency services. They're gonna send me to Healy anyway. And I obviously can't drive to Healy if I'm bleeding to death."

"That is not an emergency, Drama Queen. You're way out there, and I just smoked. I can't get pulled over again. Plus, it's raining, and I got to save gas to get to work this week. But ay—"

He chuckled, then lowered his voice in an attempt to sound seductive. "If you get that situation worked out, you can roll by. I got somethin' you can sit on, make you feel better."

I exhaled so loudly he could probably hear it. "You are worthless to me, Rome. Count on me never sitting on anything belonging to you ever again."

"That's what we doin', Vonne? Don't call me for nothin' else."

"I don't call you for nothin' in the first place. You are strictly boredom relief. Bye, Rome."

I hung up before I could cuss him six ways to Sunday. Jerome, my infrequent dick appointment, was always grumpy when he was tired and high, but I might need him in the future, so it was best not to burn that bridge yet.

My next call was to Ebony, who was equally useless. "I'm working overnights this week," she said, probably as half-asleep as she sounded. She was an office manager for a transportation company, but she picked up extra hours dispatching. In my mind, I imagined her leaned forward, her forehead on her desk, snoring away before my call came through.

"Call 911. They'll come to get you."

"You got money for an ambulance transport bill?"

"I was trying to help," Ebony snapped. "Call Daddy. He'll fuss, but he'll come to get you."

I pondered this option but ultimately decided against it. My father was a warehouse foreman who worked an early shift. He needed his rest. Besides, help from my father would be accompanied by a free lecture from my mother about how I should have planned for things like this and not need them to bail me out every time I got into trouble.

"Nah, I'm not calling Daddy. I'll figure something out."

After making several calls that went unanswered, leaving a few voicemails and sending texts that seemed to fly into the ether and go nowhere, I dropped the phone in my lap. My wound was steadily staining the silk blouse I'd used to wrap my hand.

I felt lightheaded when I stared at it, so I closed my eyes and leaned forward onto the steering wheel.

taj

"You aren't having a heart attack, Mrs. Vaughn. It's only a gas bubble. You're going to be fine."

I grasped the age-spotted hands of Loretta Vaughn, a frequent patron of Lakeside Regional Clinic, and squeezed her. Ms. Loretta was a bona fide hypochondriac who came into the clinic at least twice a week, believing she had one severe ailment or another. Tonight, she thought she was having a heart attack because she had pain in her chest.

She had also, admittedly, overeaten at dinner and it could easily be gas. So, she'd come in to check.

After giving her the usual all-clear and a sample of Gas-X strips from the medical supply, I provided her with discharge papers, which were only health care tips— she felt better when I called them discharge papers, and guided her to the cushioned chairs in the waiting room.

I squatted in front of her, so I was level with her cloudy brown eyes. "Ms. Loretta, I can't release you to walk home in the rain." She lived in the housing complex right behind the clinic, and on a clear, warm evening, I would walk her home. "I called your nephew, and he's about done with his shift. He'll come by and pick you up in a while. That okay?"

Ms. Loretta nodded as always. This had been our routine since I started working at the clinic, and she felt safe enough to keep coming back. Satisfied, I stood.

"I bet I could find some sugar cookies and a cup of decaf coffee around here if I look hard."

Her face brightened, and she smiled, revealing lipstick on her teeth. "A few cookies would be nice. I don't like to have liquids too late. I'll be up and down all night, you know."

I stepped away before she could launch into a story I did not want to hear about the frequency of bathroom trips at her advanced age. I rounded the corner from the waiting room to the nurse's station. Jaslene, my partner for the evening, rolled her eyes as I walked past her. She customarily worked day shifts, but occasionally picked up extra hours.

"Her family needs to go ahead and put her at Primrose Gardens," she muttered. "She should not be living alone, wandering around town in the rain after dark."

"She doesn't live alone. She lives with her nephew."

Jas twisted in her chair, so her knees pointed toward me and folded her arms over her chest. "And where is *his* ass? Why are we babysitting Auntie while he's out doing God knows what—"

"*Officer* Vaughn patrols Potter Lake and the highway between here and Healy. He'll drop by when he makes his way back."

Silenced, Jaslene swiveled her chair back toward the desk, running her hand through her long ponytail as she did so. I rifled through the shelves on the other side of the check-in desk, then found it: an unopened package of sugar cookies that we kept around for the diabetes patients. I ripped them open, removed two from the package, set them on a napkin, and replaced the package on the shelf.

"She still shouldn't be by herself at night."

"What do you want him to do? Chain her to the radiator? You're just mad that you almost had to do some work."

"Whatever. I heard nights at the clinic were quiet. I don't need an old lady inventing diseases and messing with my easy hours."

I playfully tapped her shoulder as I passed her again, delivered the cookies to Mrs. Vaughn, and made sure she was warm and comfortable. She bit into a cookie, her eyes glued to the monitor mounted on the wall. She liked the Home TV channel, so when she was the only person in the clinic, I indulged her. I turned up the volume and slid the remote into the empty seat next to her.

Back at the desk, I settled into my seat to finish updating Mrs. Vaughn's patient record. If she happened to come back when I wasn't on shift, which never happened because most of the staff treated her like a crazy old lady, the nurse would see my notes from this evening's treatment: Gas X and sugar cookies.

I closed down the notes program and minimized the application, revealing the computer desktop with the clinic logo across the screen. Lakeside Regional was a brand new clinic, built out of a need for a larger health care facility. Dr. Elias Moore, Potter Lake's oldest and most prominent physician, had been operating with a few partners out of an older building that hadn't met code in over a decade.

A grant from the Mayor's foundation and assistance from the state provided money to build a facility for non-emergency services and office space for Potter Lake's physicians. Life-threatening incidents were still routed to Healy General, but for the occasional scrape, regular visits, or the town hypochondriac visit, the clinic filled the hole just fine.

"This is perfect writing weather," I mused, my chin in my palm while I watched the rain splatter the windows. "I could be at the piano, listening to the storm sounds and working out some tunes."

"Mmmmm," Jaslene hummed, a perfectly arched eyebrow tipping up like I knew it would. "Or working out some*one*."

I ignored her comment and reached under the desk for my bag. We had hooked up a few times and might hook up a few times more, but I wasn't in the mood for sex-tinged banter. Besides, what made messing with Jaslene fun was sneaking around.

My nylon bag whispered softly as I pulled it from its usual hiding spot. I unearthed a spiral-bound notebook and flipped it open to the page I'd been working on earlier, its place held by my favorite pen. In my spare time, I liked to journal, write down my thoughts and feelings. Most of the time, they were just words. Other times, they turned into more.

One could say I worked in the music business, in the most behind the scenes, on-the-fringes way possible. I'd been lucky enough to write songs, ones that landed on albums and made life comfortable. Unless someone were paying close attention to the outer edges of the industry more than a decade ago, they'd never recognize my face, never know how close Taj Wright came to unimaginable fame and success.

A pair of headlights flashed past the double doors. A small coupe swerved into the lot, parked diagonally across several spaces, and screeched to a stop. Mrs. Vaughn's nephew drove a black Cadillac, so that wouldn't be him.

"Incoming," I called to Jaslene, who had left the desk and gone into the office equipment room.

"I'm busy," was her immediate response.

"Aww… did I hurt your little feelings?"

"You know what, Taj? You can fu—"

"Help! Help me, please!"

A woman stumbled through the sliding doors; one hand was wrapped in an emerald green scarf. Her hair was plastered to her head, a shock of blonde that I imagined was a nice contrast against her deep brown skin tone when it didn't resemble a dead animal.

I waved her in since she could obviously walk but was

standing just inside the door, dripping onto the mat. She rushed forward, dumping a bag on the counter in front of her.

"I slipped and fell, and I managed to slice my hand clean open and it's bleeding but I live in Healy and I wasn't sure if I should drive all that way if it's this bad—"

"Okay, okay," I interrupted, pulling up the patient application and opening a new record. "First things first. Name."

"Evonne," she chirped, spelling it out for me. "E-v-o-n-n-e . Last name Girard. This hurts like a bitch, and I think I've lost a lot of blood."

I glanced up at her arm and the dried trail from the wrist to the elbow. Then I saw the scarf, assessing that it wasn't soaked. She had probably stopped bleeding.

"You haven't lost that much blood, Miss… Girard," I finished after checking the screen. "Insurance?"

"Uhm, yeah." She dug through the bag and produced a wallet. "I was hoping you could patch me up so I could at least drive home without dripping blood everywhere."

"Sure. But first I have to get you into the system. Do you have an insurance card?"

"Can we do this *after* you stop me from bleeding to death?"

I pulled my fingers back from the keyboard, ready to give back all the attitude I was getting. But I stopped when I saw wild panic glowing in almond-shaped brown eyes and throughout the delicate features of her face. Her brows were knit together, deep wrinkles of concern across her forehead, and she was so visibly stressed, she was nearly hyperventilating.

I rolled my chair back and grabbed a clipboard already prepped with paperwork. "Leave your insurance card at the front desk and follow me. Jas?"

A grunt from the back room said she knew that I wanted her to continue processing our emotional patient into the system while I took care of the wound. I led her to an exam room, gesturing to her to hop up onto the bed—the sanitary paper crinkled under her body.

"I'm going to get some tools so I can check that out and get you stitched up."

"Thank you, doctor." She sounded relieved.

I stuck my head back around the corner. "Actually," I said, flipping my badge at her. "Taj Wright, Registered Nurse. And if you have anything slick to say about a male nurse, I will let you bleed to death. We straight?"

Meet Taj & Evonne in THE GUY NEXT DOOR, Potter Lake Book 3, now available in ebook, print and audio.

books by dl white

Find Books and Merch at Booksbydlwhite.com/shop

Brunch at Ruby's, a Ruby's novel

Dinner at Sam's, a Ruby's novel

Beach Thing, a Black Diamond Romance

Elysium, a Black Diamond Vacation Romance

The Pearl at Black Diamond, a Black Diamond Romance

Leslie's Curl & Dye, a Potter Lake Small Town Romance

Second Time Around, a Potter Lake Holiday Short

The Guy Next Door, a Potter Lake Small Town Romance

Home for the Holidays, A Potter Lake Holiday Novella

The Kwanzaa Brunch, a Holiday Short

A Thin Line

The Never List

Hey, Lover, a Second Chance Romance

Unexpected, a holiday short

The Festival at Evergreen Falls

Grumpy Valentine

Calculated Risk *(Coming Spring 2025)*

about the author

Atlanta based women's fiction and romance author DL White began seriously pursuing a writing career in 2011. She harbors a love for coffee and brunch, especially on a patio, but her true obsession is water— lakes, rivers, oceans, waterfalls! On the weekend, you'll probably find her near water and, if she's lucky, on an ocean beach.

When not writing books, she devours them. She blogs reviews and thoughts on writing and books at BooksbyDL-White.com. Grab a book by DL White and #Putitinyourface.

For more information about me/my books, visit BooksbyDLWhite.com